Love **passion** *adoration* LUST *purpose*

exploring gentle Caresse **caring** *flirty*

LOVINGLY *passionately* Stroke

feel adore COMFORT *thrust* Pleasure

explore adventure worthy **nipples**

manhood *fiery* possessive playful

tease *lustful* laughter enchanting

captivating *enhance* EROTICALLY **Love**

erotic *flirty* laughter chattering

POWERFUL **comfortable** lust *cares*

occasion ADVANTAGE excitement

Dedication

Primarily this book is dedicated to my mum for her unwavering love and support throughout every project or idea I've had over the years. You are my rock and steadfast. We have shared laughter and cried harder than anyone will ever know.

But also, to all those people who were told they were thick, stupid and would never amount to anything by individuals or role models they were encouraged to trust and look up to as a child.

Unsurprisingly this didn't instil an awful amount of confidence, self-esteem or worth in any of us.

How wrong you were to judge us.

Little apples will grow.

Acknowledgment

Thank you to all those friends and family who have listened to me go on about writing this book. For your encouragement and patience to help me cross the t's and dot the i's, I am eternally grateful to you all.

Contents

1

Blown Away

You could see his breath escaping in plumes of white clouds briefly ahead of him, before it disappeared as the biting cold stole it from his lips. He rode the steep incline of the lifeless, muddy, grass verges, littered with minuscule bouquets of purple and pink scattered heather, nuzzling between the uneven jagged rocks that sheltered there from the icy breath of the exposed highlands.

The array of clouds with their vast spectrum of greys with uneven tones, shapes and sizes, chased across the horizon, partially hiding the tired sun as it began to sink. It fell behind the mountains in the far distance, past the partly frozen babbling stream, only to leave rods of light stretching and extending out like sharply manicured fingernails trying to touch him for that final time before darkness drew the curtains of night and stopped them.

His horse was strong, not only to carry his weight but also the burden of the freshly hunted stag which lay across his neck. Still warm, its blood escaping from its wound and flicked on to his foot as it swayed back and forth when they rode. With every step they took, it splashed and scattered leaving a trail of death behind them. Ploughing on, unfaltering, sure and firm-footed, his horse became closer to the stone cottage. Not far now and he could rest.

They could see the warm inviting glow behind the hessian fabric draped across the small windows. He built it purposely that way; very slight breaks in the deep stone walls so as not to let too much of the precious warmth escape onto the harsh highlands from the open fire that burned inside. The thick, bellowing grey smoke spiralling up from the stone chimney in the centre of the roof was a sure guarantee that she would have prepared a sumptuous meal for him to return to after being exposed to a brutal day in the winter cold.

As he drew closer, he steered his horse into an outbuilding just to the side of the house where fresh bedding and blankets awaited his steed.

As he rode through the door he bowed so as not to hit his head on the low, thick, wooden beam. Once they came to a halt, he dismounted, dragging the deer with him down to the floor before heaving it across the uneven, muddy floor, leaving the scarlet trail behind it. He hoisted and placed it into a sturdy wooden casket to be cleaned and butchered later. After tying and preparing his faithful steed for the night, he secured the door. The light had finally faded as he made his way, surrounded by the quiet darkness to the heavy wooden front door of the cottage. He turned and pushed the large iron circular handle and allowed himself to enter.

The piercing brightness from the roaring fire greeted his eyes like stabbing shards of sunlight, momentarily blinding him painfully as his eyes adjusted and became accustomed to the change. Then the wall of extreme warmth hit him sharply and abruptly on his exposed, weathered face and hands forcing him to adhere to the increase in temperature.

Closing the door behind him, he saw her tending to the large pot bubbling over the raging fire, bending forward and stirring it tentatively. She heard the door shut and a brief breath of chill rushed around her hems and kissed her ankles, making her stop and glance over in his direction to see what the disturbance was. As if she didn't know already. As their eyes locked, they greeted each other with a smile, hers so much more open and freer than his tight-lipped effort. Contented and relieved that her love had returned safely from his hunt, she took the ladle out of the pot, shook off the excess, and rested it carefully by the side of the fire in the little bowl that had lived there for the entire time they had, before twisting round to face him.

She dragged both her hands down the front of her apron, wiping them to make sure they were clean before she reached around her incredibly petite waist to the small of her back to unfasten the bow and knot of her apron that had been securely holding it in place all day. She discarded it on a chair by the fire and began to walk towards him, ready to welcome her man into her arms. Her multiple layers of long skirts and petticoats swished and swayed after her and brushed the cold stone floor with a slight delay as she moved closer to greet him.

She gently approached, smiling as he unfastened his heavy skins and outer garments from his neck and shoulders. Waiting respectfully for acknowledgment, she helped him to disrobe and took his clothes from him. After all, he was her king, returning to his castle. She gazed up into his eyes flickering from one to the other like a butterfly, searching and longing to reconnect, knowing exactly what he wanted and desired as always at the end of a successful hunting day. She untangled his mountains of coats and shawls and hung them up individually over large iron hooks by the fire so they could air and dry ready for tomorrow's killing.

He walked ungracefully, heavy-footed and sluggishly unrefined, over to the large wooden calved chair positioned in front of the bed. It was draped with animal skins and blankets with a few cushions made from furs scattered over its frame. He turned round, bent and lowered himself onto the cushioned base and lent back, allowing himself to be engulfed into the soft furs, swaddled in his prizes from previous hunts, welcoming and warm to the touch. With his legs relaxed and slightly ajar, his kilt hem resting between them at his knees and laid his arms out on each arm of the chair, slumped and relaxed, he watched with anticipation, but became agitated while she fiddled and faffed, beckoning her with his eyes. He commanded her with a silent but definite finger flick gesture, wanting and waiting impatiently for his women to join him.

After carefully arranging his clothes to dry, she dutifully collected a goblet of hot broth from the fire place and presented it to him. As she leant over to place it by his side on the small table, her tightly pulled bodice allowed her voluptuous breasts to spill, provocatively showing him even more of her as it was cut so sparingly with only just enough fabric to cover her.

She could feel his breath brushing over her breasts as she retracted. Looking down, she watched him become mesmerised and bewitched by them as she paused, slightly bent in front of him. She knew too well how to tease him and he allowed her to continue with the seduction. He gazed upwards to her face once more as she mirrored his look back. Pinching and gathering her skirts and petticoats in both hands at the front, she lifted them up and away from her so as to kneel down comfortably, directly in front and as close as possible to him on the floor.

Neither one of them spoke a word, blinked or faltered from the locked trance they placed on one another as she lowered herself to her knees. Once settled, kneeling with her eyes level with his seat, still looking up, focused on his eyes, she placed both her hands on his knees. Parting his legs even more, she began to rub her hands up and under his kilt. Up from both knees, slowly and evenly, calculatingly to his thighs through his river of red coarse and tightly curled hair, to his hips, and rubbing them back down again before repeating, unhurriedly, seductively.

Bringing her hands outside his kilt and diverting her glance momentarily to untie the tight knot at his waist, she folded back the layers of tartan fabric to expose him fully. She was bursting with delight upon seeing his perfectly formed, ready-to-go, solid and strong manhood which she had been yearning for all day. It was finally in her sight and made her breath quicken with expectation of what was to come.

She fluttered a glance back up to him briefly before looking down, paying full consideration to his beast as she edged and shuffled forward, approaching it slowly, solely focused on it.

Resting one hand on his thigh, she grasped firmly but tenderly, wrapping her other hand around the enormous girth of it and levered it gently towards her mouth, applying just enough pressure with her fingers to pull it up to her, closer. In awe of it being so close, she tightened her grip and felt the pressure build with her grasp and moved her hand, pushing his skin downwards, exposing him fully. Plunging her hand into his forest of coarse auburn curly hair at the base, she slowly and gently licked him from the front to the back, skimming the tip of her tongue over his indented, vulnerable opening.

She withdrew momentarily, loosening her grip and allowing his skin to relax before continuing to massage him up and down. Retracing her steps, she repeatedly licking him as she tightened and loosened her grip, again and again pulling him down and up, over and over. Back and forth welcoming him, sucking him into her hot, cushioned, soft and inviting mouth. Pulling back with just his head inside her mouth, she sucked harder and stronger before she sucked him further, completely down towards the back of her throat, retracting, jiggling, flicking and rubbing him with her tongue and lips as he passed in and out of her mouth.

She started to gain a constant repetitive rhythm, up and down, tightening and loosening, twisting both ways as she pulled and pushed up and down, loosening and tightening her grip when she felt it necessary. She starts to lick in circles around his tip and down to the sides around his hood. Tilting her head slightly so she could glance up to her king to witness him being bewitched and enchanted by her labours to pleasure him.

With his head thrown back and his eyes closed, the ecstasy was growing inside of him, building and increasing steadily like a hunter stalking his pray. But this time, it was he who was the pray.

She places his entire beast in her mouth on the next downward push to the base of his shaft. Anchoring her hand tightly at the base she sucks even harder, moving her head up and down so he could feel himself travelling right to the very back of her throat. Feeling the warmth of her mouth, her hot saliva cascading down, warming his manhood and around her fingers, engulfing him in a heightened, excited state. Still thoroughly relishing the sensations travelling though his groin into his stomach and down to the tips of his toes, she started to become more intense, building her momentum.

Rubbing and sucking and licking, losing control faster and faster, more erratic than ever. With an overwhelming excitement of erotica, she drove faster as he started to grasp the arms of the chair firmly with his hands, knuckles shifting to white, his breathe heavier with groans escaping from his partly opened mouth becoming louder and more frequent. His groin started to twitch intensely and uncontrollably jerked and convulsed as he shot his cream into her mouth. He opened his eyes violently, straightening and locking his legs out in front of him either side of his master as she vigorously rubbed and sucked his creamy present, sucking hard and swallowing it greedily. It was her prize.

She could feel herself rocking gently from side to side, again and again content with her duty as the intensity and urgency faded. Softly and calmly, with her eyes closed, she felt a moistness escaping her mouth. Her lips quivered and made a moist flapping noise as she sucked in sharply. Startled by this sensation, she opened her eyes abruptly and blinked as she straightened her glasses before looking around, questioning where she was...

Then it became crystal-clear, looking at the elderly lady and gentleman sitting, staring straight at her with the look of horror painted across their faces. She was furthest away from the Highlands; she was travelling home from work on the 17:52 from Charing Cross to Dartford. It was lucky that she had woken up when she did as the train was just pulling into her station. Hurriedly and confused, but bizarrely content, still tingly inside from being dragged back abruptly from her dream, she came to her senses, consciously wiped her mouth with the back of her hand and collected her belongings.

Confused, feeling weak and disorientated but pleasured, she stood up and double-wrapped her scarf around her face before walking towards the exit in preparation to exit the train. She put on her gloves and held the rail waiting for the train to finish its descent. It swayed slightly side to side before finally slowly coming to a halt as she looked out of the doors into the darkness at the platform while she waited patiently for the doors to open. When they did, the ice of the winter's night wind hit her and made her hunch over as she ran out into it.

All that faced her now was the lengthy and bitingly cold walk home in the murky darkness with the relentless yearning she could feel inside her and the visions in her head of her very well-endowed king.

Maybe her king would make another social call in her dreams later tonight so she could continue the story.

2

Cooking up a Storm

She was *always* the first one home from work and, traditionally, *always* the one to start prepping the dinner. It was mid-week so the chances were he too would be home slightly early if any clients cancelled or didn't show.

The kids, on the other hand, always had after school commitments at the moment so they were always home much later than the normal school time. This gave him the very rare occasion to have her all to himself before the house was occupied with demanding voices shouting over each other, arguing amongst each other, fighting for attention.

They also brought with them an entourage of messy scatterings of textbooks, note pads, pens, pencils and maths equipment, strewn all over the entire table. All intensely grinding away, ploughing through their homework. Coming to terms with never finding the well-hidden remote control that clearly had the volume button irritatingly stuck on full, all attempts to think through the din of a music channel were banished.

He desperately endeavoured to hold onto the shreds of sanity, reminiscing how very different it was now the teen years had arrived compared to the calmer less rowdy younger years when they treasured cuddles and bedtime stories. The kids being tucked up, bathed and in bed by 7pm, asleep by 7:15pm, seemed to be a very distant memory, never to return.

She was already at the hob busy stirring pots of simmering vegetables as the pie had been in the oven for well over 30 minutes and was browning beautifully. He paused for a moment and steadily took a deep, controlled breath out so as to completely concentrate and compose himself as he deliberated what was in store for him. Putting his key in the lock and turning it as quietly as he possibly could, he cringed and held his breathe as the lock clicked slightly as it unlocked. He didn't want to make his presence known but sought the element of surprise as he cautiously pushed the door open.

Yes, he thought to himself proudly as he pulled the key back out of the lock and delicately placed one foot in front of the other, squeezing passed the front door without being noticed. Holding the handle down, he closed the front door behind him and in double slow motion let the handle spring back up and rest in its natural position without making any sound so as not to disturb her.

He softly crept on tiptoe through the hall and lounge, out into the kitchen where he paused to take a deep breath while he ogled her. There she was, a vision of beauty even if she was just cooking dinner. He was in awe, almost drooling, staring at her perfectly toned ass. He bent and quietly placed his bag down in the doorway, cautious not to be noticed, or to disturb her.

He silently approached her from behind, raising his arms in front of him ready to capture her waist with his outstretched fingers before his body would engage contact. Touch down; he'd made contact. Guiding and wiggling his fingers first, then his hands, he pulled himself into her space, sweeping and wrapping his arms around to her front as he moved his body closer and colliding politely but firmly as he pushed his groin up against her bottom firmly. Linking his arms at her front, he squeezed his bulging arms like steel clamps around her waist, ever so tenderly so as not to hurt her, but to hold her securely. Her protector, her rock, her hero was home.

She grasped her delicate hand over the top of his forearms, nowhere near the size or as solid as his, and relaxed, holding them there with reassurance and comfort. He rocked and swayed her from side to side lovingly as he buried his head into the side of her elegant long neck, inhaling the faded perfume she had spritzed there earlier that morning before going to work. Totally the opposite of his cologne, which had just been freshly applied. It teased her senses as it swept around to greet her, making her nose tingle with excitement. He had just come straight from the gym so had the chance to freshly shower and had reapplied it just for her benefit. He truly smelt gorgeous. *I guess it's one of the perks being a professional boxer; you can freshen up before you leave the office,* she thought.

He respectfully released one of his heavy clamps, brushed aside her long golden hair to reveal more of her neck so he could smother her with tender, open-mouthed kisses, too which she didn't object. In fact, she aided his quest and surrendered herself by leaning her head over even more sideways in the other direction so he could gain greater access and be even more accurate with his additional kisses, on even more of her neck. Planting them right on the spots where he knew she loved it, sending shivers down her spine, making her crave and want him immediately, right away, right there, right now.

She froze in motion so as not to disturb his rhythm, closed her eyes and erased any thoughts of dinner. Instead, she filled her mind with only visions of him, erotic visions, uncensored, of how she could and would pleasure him and be pleasured by him in return, fulfilling her fantasies. While she was still securely held by one of his clamps, he drew his attention to her front with his free hand. He brushed down her side, under her arm, over her belly and further down her front to her pelvis. He could feel her warm, soft and inviting groin even through her skirt that was in his way, stopping him from being raw skin-to-skin as it tugged around her thighs as he tried to reach underneath, longing to nestle his hand between her legs and cup her firmly.

She could feel him underneath her, drawing his palm and fingers in, pressing on her pelvis through the fabric as if he was trying to break and burrow through her clothes. With his thumb outside, she could feel him squeeze it towards his fingers, trying to force them together but her skirt proved stronger. All the while he was open-mouth kissing her, nibbling and biting at her neck, heightening her senses and arousing her even more.

She too was searching her way up and over her shoulder, behind her head, to caress and stroke the side of his face with one hand then released her other hand to caress his shoulder and neck on the other side while his continued to ravenously kiss, developing more wild and savage behaviour.

Now with her hands distracted and no longer a hindrance, it gave him the advantage to unclamp his other arm and steer it up to find her breast. He felt his way up outside of her shirt and cradled the whole of her breast in his hand. First squeezing and then moving it firmly around and around so she could feel the tug of lust through her bra and clothes. Biting down on her lip she became more aroused. She didn't want to deny herself from kissing his lips any longer, so she started to turn round, intensifying the tug to her body. He released his grip just enough so she could move with ease to position herself to face him and then straight away drew her nearer, so their bodies collided once more, pressing into each other, this time with more urgency. She looked up and kissed him delicately at first, with finesse and control, but this soon developed into uncontrollable firmer kisses. Her tongue seductively gained full access to every part inside his mouth, biting his lip and teasing him as she withdrew and then returned for more.

Holding the sides of his face with her hands, she moved her lips away from his mouth and began to explore down his neck, over his shoulders and across his chest. She swirled her hands around the torso she had felt a million times, but the need to touch him was just too overwhelming. He bought his hands up past her waist, grabbing and clenching at her shirt, rubbing and stroking her back, down past her waist to her bottom, squeezing and releasing it.

He dragged her skirt again, clasping his hand between and under her bottom cheeks, pulling her away from the hob towards him passionately, pressing his groin into hers. She could feel his solid monster through the fabric up against her again.

He released his grip and crouched slightly to glide his hands from her waist down to her hips and each side of her outer thighs, stopping at the hem of her floral short A-line skirt. He slipped both hands under the skirt and began to raise them back up her body, skin on skin, hitching her skirt as he went. He rose his hands back up her outer thigh, high enough so his thumbs could reach the tops of her knickers while kissing her continuously, like he was playing a game, trying to distract her, diverting her attention from his real intentions. But she knew exactly what he was doing and loved every second of the seduction but pretended she had no idea and played along, secretly wanting it even more than he did.

He bent his thumbs and hooked them over the top of her smooth satin underwear and mercifully began to pull them down with precision and conviction but being gentle so as not to hurt or mark his precious goddess in anyway. As they travelled over her hips and to her thighs, they became less resistant. He unhooked his thumbs and allowed them to fall, gracefully cascading down her slightly opened legs to the floor, effortlessly resting at her ankles where she stepped out of them one foot at a time before brushing them away to one side with her toes.

Now exposed for him to pleasure her further, free of any barriers between them apart from his trousers, she unbuckled his belt and started to undress and loosen his clothing while he hurriedly began to explore her body once more. As they stood, bodies pressed up against each other, face to face, he manoeuvred his hand down once more, in between her opened legs further this time.

He could truly feel her warmth radiating as he freely slid his fingers and palm down under her soft, shaved and inviting pussy. He felt past her hood and slid his fingers down her centre until his splayed thump buffered up against her leg, bringing his hand to a stop. He didn't mind this as he knew his fingers were in exactly the right position to give him full access to enter inside her and to pleasure her before he pleasured himself.

He angled, raised and drummed all his fingers one after the other as he began to press further towards her opening. Rubbing backwards and forwards as his initiated steady progress, alternating the pressure between his three middle fingers before gently angling and hooking his middle finger slightly forward and upwards. He had pushed through her barrier and could feel the intense wetness inside her.

He began to guide his finger blindly up slowly at first but then deeper inside her. Feeling her tightness and stickiness surround him before retracting it slightly and repeating the motion, rubbing her back and forth.

She could feel him travelling up inside, deeper each time, rubbing his finger in and out of her. Then she felt another finger being inserted inside her, joining his other well established lubricated middle finger. It was dry at first but soon became just as lubricated as the first. She was so horny and wet with her natural love juice thanks to him making her feel so sexy and desired. She could feel him rubbing back and forth inside, over her G-spot, and his thumb outside rubbing and caressing her hood and clit.

While he was concentrating on pleasuring her, she was equally concentrating on him and had freed him from the burden of his trousers, rubbing, showing focused attention, starting to make him even harder and throb more while they were still locked, mouth-to-mouth, wrestling, tugging and tussling tongues.

He retracted his lubricated fingers from inside her, parting and slowly wiping them all over her labia and over her hood so her juices spread out all over and around her. He held her firmly and lifted her body, elevating her just above his now fully erect monster. She raised her legs up, circled and locked them around his hips, drawing him closer. Steadily and accurately, he aligned his head underneath her wet opening and began to lower her gently on to his hard, throbbing manhood.

Already lubricated, her lips opened effortlessly, slipped and surrounded him fully until her hood fell to meet his groin where he couldn't penetrate her any deeper. She was perched on the edge of the worked surface, and as she felt his entirety right up inside of her, it made her gasp out loud. She couldn't swallow any more of his magnificence. He retracted himself only to push and thrust back up inside her, deeper and harder, over and over, slow at first but increasing the intensity with each thrust. She was so hungry for his love she greedily accepted everything he wanted to give her. Then, suddenly, they heard the front door slam.

Alarmed at the unexpected sound of intruders, hurriedly and abruptly they wrenched themselves apart, panicking, unaware of who it could be as no one was scheduled to be home, no one, absolutely *no one*. Both felt cheated, resentful and short-changed. She hastily pulled her skirt back down from her waist, straightened out her crumpled blouse and ruffled hair and turned to face the hob to resume her position, breathing heavy, flustered and flushed. He pulled up his trousers that had fallen to the floor, fastened them quickly with the button first as he exasperated his energy and failed miserably to hide, or take control of his full erection. Battling and wrestling to put it back in its box, he struggled to control the slipperiness of it, growing increasingly concerned as to whose footsteps and voices he could hear. The muttering travelled through the living room, fast approaching the kitchen door, totally unaware of what they could potentially be walking into. Finally, he was able to close his fly just as their daughter walked into the kitchen with a study friend, Karolanne, from school.

Throwing her bag uncaringly on the kitchen table, rolling her eyes as she lazily dragged her feet towards the fridge, she announced, 'Hockey practice was cancelled.' She opened the fridge door sharply, wrenched two bottles of juice from the bottom shelf before slamming the door shut again with the bottom of one of the bottles. She handed one to Karolanne who observed them standing with both their backs to the girls, staring at the wall, breathing erratically. The girls walked back in to the living room, made themselves comfortable, turned the television on full volume and relaxed.

She looked down at the floor to see her discarded knickers scrunched up in a heap in the middle of the kitchen for all to see. She hurriedly scooped then up and hid them in her pocket as he softly put his arm around her, pulled her close to him as he kissed her on the forehead before saying, 'Maybe later, beautiful.'

It looked like dinner *was* going to be the only thing to be cooking in the kitchen that night after all.

3

Lick and Suck

He stood there, leaning into her, forcefully restraining her up against the wall with the lower half of his body pushed up tight against hers. He delicately kissed her voluptuous and luxurious lips. With his eyes closed softly, blindly he embarked on unbuttoning her cream, waterfall chiffon long-sleeved blouse, just enough to brush it with both hands over her shoulders, guiding it down, free from her arms.

The top of her body was now mostly unwrapped as the fabric of her blouse draped untidily but gently cascaded around her hips with its hem still being partially snaggled and tucked in to her skirt at the waist. The top half of her large, pert breasts were entirely exposed for his pleasure, and despite the lower half being cradled and protected in a mixture of pure white lace and satin balcony bra, he could still caress and play.

With lips locked and only retracting momentarily to change position of tongue, they persistently and relentlessly explored each other's open mouths, arching and angling their heads from side to side as they hurriedly ventured further into each other, psychologically knowing they didn't have much time.

They could faintly hear the disturbance of people outside the locked door, slightly muffled at times, jumbled and blurred. Trivial conversations, increasing and decreasing in volume as they came closer, walked by and then faintly drifting into the distance, before finally disappearing altogether as they walked down the length of the corridor, disappearing through doors into their own designated offices.

After the slight distractions, she felt her way around to his back, through his shirt and connected with the warmth and presence of his excitement, feeling his pounding heart as she rested her hand on his firm, toned chest.

Blindly, as this was all he could do, he reached out delicately but with more confidence, finding his way to the top of her bra, touching her bare flesh for the first time. He couldn't believe how soft and warm she was as he tentatively brushed his fingertips across the top of the lace fringe and around to the back, seeking out its security clasp. With stealth-like precision and accuracy, he found it with one hand, and with his other around the opposite side of her body, he joined and united them together to make contact and figured out a strategy to free her breasts from their cages of lace and satin.

With both sides of the bra secured in each respected hand, he politely squeezed the eyelets together being careful not to pinch her soft delicate skin between them. Once he felt the eyelet become unhooked, he supported both sides of the bra while they retracted and parted from each other. The bra gradually loosened its hold on her breasts, and they were freed from their elevated prison of structured lace silk and wires.

As he released his grip, the bra fell to the floor, whereas her breasts, on the other hand, stayed true to form and shape. They did not falter from their posts, but stood proud and poised, pert to attention, nevertheless naked, looking up at him, waiting for the next encounter of his tender caress. With them, both exposed totally for his pleasure, mesmerised by their glory, he struggled to decide which one to pay his attention to first now they were unrestricted and giving him permission and unlimited access.

He held them both, one in each hand, as he bent slightly to his right and with the very tip of his tongue began to tease her. He gently licking the very tip of one of her pert, hard, erect nipples, deliberately missing it on occasions as he brushed past it so delicately.

So as not to leave her other breast waiting in anticipation for his lust and attention, he brushed his thumb across her nipple and cradled her other breast. Tentatively playing, moving his thumb in circles making her other attribute even more erect, while it waited patiently for the attention of the gentle flick of his tongue. He continued to conquer, more precise and firmly, rolling around her nipple in circular motion, one way then the other, softly at first before covering the whole nipple. He then drew it into his slightly opened mouth, while stroking it with his tongue, air-tight and totally encapsulated.

He sucked in short but meaningful bursts before biting and pulling himself away gently from her, letting her escape from his mouth, only to then be guided and drawn back in stronger. Each time, back and forth, harder and firmer while caressing her twinned nipple, twisting it in between his fingers and thumb the whole time, rolling and feeling it grow in heat and friction as he steadily applied more and more pressure. She was condemned, influenced by his enchantment and power of seduction.

Squeezing... squeezing, conditioning it ready for his mouth to make it as equally erect after he had exhausted her left breast. After sucking it sharply, he narrowed his mouth yet again so she could feel his teeth holding on to her firmly. Her breast was lubricated from his saliva, letting him slide easily over her, heightening her want for him sexually.

With excited electric tremors sending shockwaves through her body, she was becoming exhausted with anticipation and delight, feeling herself weakening from his touch. Her eyes where wide open but unable to see any shadows in the wall of darkness. She looked upwards as if there would be stars, stars to cast light, any light at all so she could have some reassurance that she wasn't fantasizing or making it up and he was actually there with her.

Looking hurriedly around her, she hunted for some glow of light in this closed, confined space. Something from anywhere, a miniscule glimmer of light from the crack in the door so as to show him to her would have been welcomed and pleasuring for her. Defeated in the search, she closed her eyes once more as her efforts were impractical and unrealistic. So she concentrated her attention on reaching out for the side of his head as touch was the only sense she had at her disposal and true confirmation that they were there. Suddenly she was given a gift, a gift from someone's text. As the soft light illuminated and escaped from her phone screen that was tucked in her front pocket of her skirt, it gave her just a faint hint of his silhouette as it shone across the room and bounced off the opposite wall. He was now available in the inkiness and made her feel complete.

Suddenly, with no warning, the door handle tilled down and upwards sharply and repeatedly three or four times as someone was trying to open it. Their passion was halted abruptly. She gasped as they swiftly broke free and pushed away from each other, scared they may be caught. He stood there, vulnerably exposed, his tightly stretched trousers across his immense and incredibly large erect manhood, bulging. Her, even more so, with no clothes on the top half of her body. They both stood there frozen in motion like rabbits caught in the headlights, unsure as to what to do next. Where could they run to? Simple answer to that question. Nowhere, they were trapped.

All they could do was wait in silence, pray that whoever was trying to open the door went away and hoped they didn't go and get the skeleton key from reception. So they froze in silence before finding the courage to fumble sightlessly, reaching out to each other to hold hands for comfort and solidarity. Thankfully, the door failed to open.

Relieved, they remembered they had locked it from the inside.

He began to fidget nervously. Slightly uncomfortable, he needed to re-adjust himself to relieve the tightness and strangulation of his manhood. 'Shush,' she muttered quietly as she pressed her fingers accurately and tentatively against his lips before the light from her phone extinguished itself and eventually faded and died.

She was worried. She was *very* worried. If anyone had managed to walk in, they would have both been dismissed immediately. After all, they were taking refuge at work in the stationary cupboard. It was 10:30am and she had only just left her office to make the boss his cup of coffee for morning breaktime.

'Where the Fuck is she? Where's Sophie?' he roared crossly, scowling at everyone he passed in the corridor. 'Where the Fuck is my coffee?'

The boss had only been waiting for five minutes, becoming more anxious and agitated with ever second that passed, waiting for his caffeine fix. His larger than average frame breathed heavily before turning and stomping away from the door, continuing to bellow his dislikes as he trudged down the corridor aggressively pushing both the doors open at the end harshly.

As they heard the footsteps become fainter, they began to come back down to reality. Sophie hurriedly redressed herself, refastening her bra, threading her arms back through her sleeves, tugging her blouse over her shoulders before buttoned it up at the front in a frenzy. *Quickly, quickly,* she thought, *get dressed.* She had to get dressed, out the stockroom and into the staffroom to make his coffee before he came back to hunt her down again.

Once more slightly composed, they both paused and looked at each other. Breathing erratically, trying to catch and control the situation, he started to unlock the door, one notch on each exhalation, checking to see he was mirroring her actions. Slowly and calmly, she turned the handle and instigated the opening of the door cautiously, unaware of what could potentially be waiting for them on the other side.

The light shone through the gap of the door as she slowly and unhurriedly opened it further, checking that no one was directly outside. Then nervously she took the lead and sculked out, followed closely by Glenn. They stood side by side, holding hands, looked at each other and parted with a smile as they let go to walk in opposite directions down the corridor. They knew neither of them got what they really wanted but just a taster of what could possibly be the start of an electrifying, hot and steamy office romance.

As Sophie walked away, longing for his touch, she looked back over her shoulder before she smoothed down her skirt and re-adjusted her breasts in her bra through her blouse. Profoundly, she pondered on the notion, thinking to herself as she pushed the door of the staffroom open. *Note to self, make the boss his coffee first before embarking on any activity next time with the clear understand that there's always lunch time to partake in any lengthier encounters in the foreseeable future.*

4

A Warm Welcome

He was in the bathroom and had been for what seemed like an eternity but, in reality, it was only about 25 minutes. She opened the front door gently and closed it softly behind her by leaning back up against it with her bottom. She could hear the shower running and the water in the distance behind the closed door, delicately drumming rhythmically on the base of the shower tray. It was repetitive and relentless, like a steady stream, as the water ran off his body. The rest of the house stood in deathly silence. He hadn't even turned the tv on or the radio when he got in from work but headed straight for the bathroom that evening.

She tenderly peeled off her coat and draped it casually but peacefully on the coat hook at the base of the stairs, flicked off her clumpy work shoes carelessly, leaving them haphazardly laying wherever they fell, half in and half out of the hallway and lounge. This permitted her to pad bare foot and on tippy-toes up the staircase without being detected or drawing attention to herself. She unbuttoned her blouse hurriedly as she went, but as quietly as she could, just in case he heard any disturbance. If he would have known she was home, that would ruin the surprise she had planned.

She eventually reached the top of the stairs, breathing slightly heavier now, not knowing if it was the assent or the excitement and element of surprise she was feeling that made her a little breathless. The bathroom door was tightly closed, so she carefully walked past, quietly concentrating on trying to control and slow down her breathing. Making her way gingerly further across the landing to the bedroom in complete silence, she tugged and pulled her blouse over her wrists and head as some of the buttons stubbornly refused to detach themselves from their buttonholes.

She entered the bedroom, discarding and peeling herself from her remaining clothes, dragging and fighting them with a sense of urgency. Once free, she finally laying them to rest over the back of the dressing table chair where they hung lifelessly and unorganised.

Light-headed and dizzy, bubbling with excitement, knowing she was going to join him soon, she unhooked her bra and allowed her breasts to escape from the shackles they had endured for the entire day. With both hands she tenderly massaged around and underneath them as they revelled in their freedom before she flipped her attention and started to pull down her knickers and wriggled out of them. She allowed them to fall to the floor and stepped out of them before heading back across the landing once more. Now totally naked, she paused outside the bathroom door.

Placing her hand on the handle, she rested and delayed turning it for a moment. She needed a few moments just to be allowed to compose herself before going in, as she knew pleasure wasn't far away. It was just waiting for her to arrive on the other side of the door where she would present herself to him.

With both excitement and anticipation bubbling in her stomach and deep down inside, she fought tirelessly to control her emotions before leisurely pushing down fully on the handle. Slowly and with composure, she pushed the door forward unhurriedly, creating the slightest of cracks in between the frame and the door so as to be nosy and pry. With her face close, tightly resting against the door, she could secretly spy on him but was only able to see through the opening she had created with one eye. As she continued to edge the door open further, she was greeted with a warm wall of moisture and mist annoyingly attempting to break free from the bathroom, slipping through the ever-increasing crack in the doorway.

She tried not to allow too much steam to escape as this was her screen and would blow her cover if he saw her beyond it. She passed through the door sideways hastily and closed the door as promptly as she possibly could behind her. First mission accomplished.

Pleased with herself for entering the room without being noticed, she stood there briefly so her lungs could adjust to the perfumed, moist, dense air that was now touched every exposed surface of her body. Looking forward, she allowed herself to be engulfed into her surroundings. She could just make out his silhouette. He stood there in the mist, naked behind the full length, translucent, glass shower screen. Standing motionless, like a statue, facing the wall, with his eyes closed, the showerhead rose directly above him with his back towards her. His arms were outstretched to the side, suspended like a bridge at shoulder hight, one hand anchored against the wall and the other one on the shower screen, he was unaware of her being in attendance, standing still behind him, or of what her intentions were.

He had been standing there motionless for some time. The water ran down and cascaded onto his now slightly bowed down-turned head. It flowed like torrents of water being poured, all over his neck and down his back. Downwards, either finding the crevasses of his proud muscles on his back to travel all the way down to his feet or bouncing off of his smooth rocky chest and arm muscles, hitting the tiled wall or glass screen. The glass became overwhelmed with beads of water clinging on for dear life. Helplessly they began to fall and flow hurriedly downwards to be reunited with the other droplets now swimming and forming a lake in the shower tray, engulfing and surrounding his feet.

The droplets that clung to the celling grew larger and heavy until they were bulbous globules being stretched before finally surrendering to gravity. When they could no longer hold on, they released themselves and tumbled downwards by the pull. So, like individual missiles carelessly free-falling, they began to land on anything that happened to be in their path beneath them.

Naked, she carefully walked to him, desperate not to disturb his concentration while he stood there, still, exposed and vulnerable, allowing himself to be rained on and consumed by the warm, soothing water. Steadying herself with one hand on the shower screen, she stepped into the large porcelain tray to join him. She unhurriedly laid her other hand with outspread fingers on his muscular back at his shoulder as the water reached out and started to rain on her too.

Now she had brought herself to his attention, he calmly awakened from his stupor, opened his eyes, and gracefully turned himself around to face her. He wrapped his drenched arm around her partly dry waist and drew her in to join him under the showerhead. Her curved, landscaped figure could also now be drenched by the warm flow of water.

Their bodies connected, their lips delicately kissing each other through the wall of water, their fingertips and hands familiarising themselves with each other's body as they had been denied each other's touch since this morning. Holding him close, she began to explore more, moving her hands under his arms and around to the top of his back, spreading her fingers before softly applying the gentlest of pressure before running and chased her nails sympathetically down his entire back to his bottom, then once again drawing him in closer. She could feel him growing as he became harder, moving upwards, brushing past her inner thighs in between her legs as it woke from his watery coma. It pressed upwards against her wet, drenched pussy as it could not elevate any higher.

He too started to explore around her back, at her waist first before extending his reach up and downwards with his hands, massaging her soft skin as he became aroused by the gentle pressure of her nails running down his back.

She started kissing his neck before she momentarily stepped backwards and randomly began to kiss his chest and lick his nipples, all the time massaging him. She steadily moved her kisses down towards his stomach as she positioned herself and knelt in front of him. Looking directly at his outstanding manhood, she struggled to contain him in one hand as he was exceptionally well-endowed with the widest girth she had ever been privy too.

Slowly she adjusted her grip on him and bought him towards her mouth. As he looked down at her, she gently licked and sucked at the end of him, teasing, readjusting her grip, hauling him back and forth with one hand while cradling his balls in her other hand. He watched the temptress at work with this act of teasing just before she opened her warm moist mouth and allowed him to enter her, right to the very back of her throat.

Moving her head towards his groin, mouth stretched open wide with her hand still holding him around his base she fought to take his total, full, out-stretched length in her soft, hot velvety mouth all at once. She tilted and angled her head back slightly which helped her throat open so she could take the last of him inside her. She achieved this with such grace as she always did. Another mission accomplished.

Now, he took command. He was in control of the motion as she allowed him to thrust himself forward into her mouth while she started to massage underneath him. Surrendering and supporting his action, she took her other hand away and gently positioned it on one hip, guiding him back and forth, in and out of her mouth with each of his thrusts.

Now it was her turn to take the lead and be in control once more. She moved her other hand away from underneath him so she could grasp both his hips and squeezed them as she began to suck him into her. She felt him push himself, reaching down deep into her throat while holding and supporting the back of her head.

Droplets of water still trickled down over his toned body, flowing and splashing onto her upturned face, making it impossible for her to open her eyes. Now blinded by the force of the harsh slashing water, she was unable to open her eyes to see his face. But she could tell that he was about to cum, as he had picked up the speed of his thrusting and his footing had started to falter with exhilarating excitement.

Feeling her way and holding him again, tighter this time, she gently took command back and bought him outside, releasing him from her mouth but still rubbing and massaging him up and down his shaft. He started to contract and convulse, pumping his creamy milk all over her breasts. Some slid and slipped down her cleavage over her abs, trickling down over her pussy only to be lost down her thigh to her knees and then escaping her body into the shower. He scooped some up in his hands and smoothly rubbed it over her breasts as he squeezed and tugged them.

After a time, his milk was mixed and was eventually diluted by the water until it totally disappeared, as if it had never even been there at all. His heart rate regained normal pace as he helped her to her feet. Holding her closely, secure in his arms, he leant down, giving her delicate open kisses to her face and neck before whispered tenderly in her ear, 'Now it's your turn!'

5

Prince Charming

The Stag's Head was way too convenient, being a stone's throw away from the staff entrance that they all spilled out of when the shop lights lowered their glare, the tills had been cashed up and the security guard had made his final sweep.

They all – the girls and boys from the yard – excitedly, boisterously and noisily laughed and joked as they made their way hurriedly across the back car park to satisfy their long-awaited craving of a pint or short after a long day of having to behave themselves, adhering to the rules and regulations of the protocol they called, work.

Some were able to quench one of their long-awaited cravings immediately after stepping out of the building by sparking up and lengthily inhaling on a cigarette, feeling the flame from the lighter being drawn through so the heat could hit the back of their throat. The smell of smoke filled and twirled through the air as they walked, leaving a trail behind them of gently swirling and dancing smoke, rising through the invisible current before lazily evaporating into the early summers evening sky that was awash with scattered clouds, brushed by the soft setting sun. Faded pastel pinks, orange, blues and purples all merged together like plumes of multicoloured candy floss bagged at the fun fair being hauled gently and leisurely across the sky.

As tired as they were, they were in need of refreshments to recharge the batteries as the sun dropped unhurriedly – not that they took any notice. They walked to the corner entrance which always had both doors wedged open even in torrential rain with makeshift doorstops created from folded up beer mats that sat on all the tables. Genius, Iceberg and blue Stripe seemed to be the favourable, along with Mightily Arrow or whichever ones the rep left that week that should have been used for promotional purposes. They always had multiple purposes and were the most effective door stops or table levellers, only being replaced when they buckled or became flattened from the weight of the tables or doors pushing up against them or by being lost at last orders when they were kicked out of the way so the doors could be closed and locked for the night. The aroma of beer enticed and welcomed them in as they approached, promising an evening of replenishment and relaxation for all.

He strolled confidently up to the bar with the guys as he did every Friday and Saturday evening after finishing work. He stood proudly while scanning and searching eagerly from left to right, trying to get someone's attention from the other side of the bar. He needed to have a drink poured for him to quench his thirst and fill his tastebuds with anything alcoholic so he could finally draw a definitive line between work and play time. He stood there patiently waiting to be served, tired, still in his white but wrinkled shirt he had been wearing all day, complete with the dirty scuff marks drawn by the masses he had been manually lifting on his shoulders and back. His shirt tail scruffily hung down on one side.

He wasn't paying too much attention to what or who was behind him until he saw her walk through the double doors. She was a few minutes late as she had to go home to change before meeting them. The landlord would not have appreciated a girl in his pub on a Friday evening still dressed in her school uniform. Even though she attended the sixth form college and in her final year, they still insisted on them wearing their full uniform.

It wasn't a look she was enamoured with either. All freshly changed, she saw him there and immediately felt butterflies rising inside her. He stood like an iconic statue as she walked over to join him. He was naturally tanned, muscles on muscles, strong broad shoulders and a dizzy towering height of six-foot-three, with thick black curly hair. She moved toward him secretly, she thought, from behind, not wanting to disturb him until he would feel the touch of her hand threading its way around his waist to hug him close. Like a lioness stalking her pray, she moved closer, ready to pounce. But she was going to be scuppered. He was standing, directly facing the highly polished mirrored wall in front of him that backed the bar where the spirits sat waiting to be selected. He saw his goddess's reflection as soon as she walked through the doors and could see her attempt to stalk him.

As she was a hair's breadth away, he turned and held his arms out to her, ready to capture this beautiful creature and invite her into his grasp to hold her close to his body. He had been thinking about her erotically, missing her all day. As their bodies collided and he gently received her, securely drawing her in and holding her close, one arm fixed around her waist with his other exploring and gliding over her back. He caressed and cradled her in his sturdy arms while silently reconnecting, planting kisses all over her face and neck, making her laugh out loud, while inhaling her fresh perfume with thoughts of passion frantically chasing through his mind despite his composed exterior as he concentrated on being the true gentleman he was.

He flirtatiously gave her neck open-mouthed kisses, delicately licking and tasting her skin before pulling his body away but still entrapping her in his grasp at her tiny waist. He lingered and gazed deep into her soul, which was pure and innocent, through her eyes of crystal emerald green edged with the longest thick eyelashes, reaching out and flickering seductively on each blink, unaware of the turmoil they created.

He studied and inspected her entire face with its complexion as clear, smooth and refined as porcelain, the delicate scattering of freckles on her nose, which he adored. It almost looked as if he was counting them one by one to make sure none were missing as he brushed his hand across her cheek. He twirled her long chestnut hair, winding its bouncing curls around his fore finger before pulling it towards his nose and taking a deep breath to engulf its sweet fragrance, all the time absorbed into her eyes.

She returned the unhurried glance upwards to his creamy dark chocolatey eyes and was ensnared by his striking looks. His soft, blemish-free and flawless darkened skin from his Spanish heritage made her blush with excitement and anticipation. She was utterly astounded that he wanted to be with her; she felt as if she was the luckiest girl alive. He could have anyone, but he wanted her.

Eventually they were teased and told to "put each other down" by everyone else so they did and continued to be close, stood side by side, playing and giggling at the bar, still waiting to be served. She stayed snuggled in close, softly nestled underneath his arm as he casually cuddled her, resting his hand over her shoulder. They were a perfect fit with her arm resting delicately and reassuringly around his waist as she never, ever wanted to let him go.

With endless chattering, laughing and joking together, alongside the relentless feeding of the pool table with the fifty pence pieces that were continuously lined up like soldiers on parade down one side of the table, before being fed through the slot one by one, the evening passed by so quickly.

The sun eventually slipped away leaving darkness with only pin holes of light from the stars above, far in the distance, shimmering down observing as they left after the last bell was rung. They headed home, all going their own separate ways more quietly now as they had satisfied their thirst for food, drink and socialising.

Inseparable as they had been all night, arm in arm they walked along the high street not needing to pay any attention to the pavement as he had walked her home so many times before. They could do it literally with their eyes closed. As they walked up the hill to her house, she noticed the car had gone; her parents weren't home, they too were out for the evening with their friends. This was really unusual, a rarity to come home and have the whole house to herself. So she invited him in rather than the usual kissing and warm long goodnight cuddles outside on the doorstep before he walked home alone.

She clasped his hand tightly, nervous she may somehow loose him. She never wanted to be separated from him, she adored him. He made her feel like no one else has ever made her feel. With his hand in hers, she turned the key in the lock and pushed the door open. Taking the lead, she walked through the open doorway while glancing back at him over her shoulder, smiling as he followed. She turned, not letting go of his hand and guided him through before shutting the door securely behind them and they stood in the hallway facing each other.

She tossed her keys into the bowl on the small table so she could pay him her full attention, play and explore with her hands while their lips locked together. They enjoyed the uninterrupted intimacy with no one around before she paused momentarily to question herself: was she doing the right or wrong thing? She always struggled with letting her emotions show as they were, in the past she was always betrayed. But he was so different from any boyfriend she had had in the past. It was time, she just knew he was the one and she wanted him, so she held his hand once more and led him up the stairs to her bedroom. Increasingly scared to let go, she held his hand more firmly than ever as she guided him in through the bedroom door and closed it quietly behind him. She had him at last in her bedroom but was still uncertain that his feelings were as strong or as genuine as hers.

She knew what she wanted but was unsure of how to ask for it or how to instigate it. What should she do next? She'd never done this before. She looked down, shy, and awkwardly started to pull up and free her t-shirt from her skirt. Crossing her arms, she pulled it slowly over her head before straightening it out and placed it at the bottom of her bed. She reached round to the back of her skirt and began to unzip it and shuffled it down her legs before stepping out of it and placing it beside her t-shirt.

He stood there silently, observing her gracefully undress herself in front of him until she was only wearing her bra and knickers. She felt exposed but continued, turning her attention now to his shirt. Starting at the top and working her way down, she delicately unbuttoned it, one button at a time, slowly and methodically until they were all free from their buttonholes and the shirt was allowed to gape, exposing the centre of his sculptured body and curves of his chest.

She brushed her fingertips sensually down his front and under the shirt before moving and rubbing her hands from his waist to his solid abs, past his polished chest, up and over his shoulders. Pushing the shirt backwards, it loosened and began to fall down his arms and away from his body, lifelessly landing on the floor in a heap. She rested the side of her head on his naked chest as she clutched her hands around his waist and felt his heartbeat racing inside as she held him securely. He returned the gesture and wrapped his arms around her bare shoulders. She could feel him hard against her through his trousers.

The tension was overwhelming, growing stronger by the second, stirring around inside them both like a hurricane building momentum, both knowing only too well she was an unspoilt fruit, untouched by any man or boy. They peeled themselves back away from each other, trying to fight the feeling that raged inside and stood clenching hands, looking longingly into each other's eyes, knowing it felt so right and this could be the point of no return. That moment of hysteria began to fade as the seconds ticked away and developed into minutes. He was deep in private thoughts only to decide to loosen his grip and pull his hands away from her, allowing hers to drop to her sides where they hung thinking he was disappointed and she had been rejected.

He stood there fighting with his morals and beliefs, weighing up his options and conclusions to his potential actions, making a decision that could and would change their entire relationship by taking it to the next step. He was with no doubt deeply in love with her and had been for the last 6 months they had been going out together for. But as ever the gentleman, he didn't want to put pressure on her and that's why he would wait for her. It would be her decision alone to make and no one else's. He seemed distant, out of reach but standing right in front of her. She felt ashamed and now flushed with embarrassment. Her bottom lip started to quiver and her breathing became short with anxiety as her eyes welled with tears.

She didn't want to wait any longer, she wanted him now, she's always wanted him. From the very moment she saw him, she's knew he was the one and she had waited for over six months thinking about it and didn't want to wait any longer. It was killing her inside, the thought of not having him.

As she leant forward to pick up her t-shirt to redress herself, he caught her by her wrist and delicately removed the shirt from her hand and placed it back on to the bed. He took hold of his belt with both hands and started to unfasten it, releasing it from the eyelet and continued to finish taking off the rest of his clothes before standing there naked for her to witness him bare and vulnerable. He was open to her judgement and choice as to whether she wanted to continue down this road they both yearned for, but only if she wanted to.

Naked, he looked at her tear-welled eyes and wiped them dry and stood there waiting patiently for her to make the next move, whatever that would be. She composed herself before she reached around to unfasten her bra and slipped her knickers down her thighs before stepping out of them.

Now they both stood there, face to face, once more totally naked, just looking and enjoying the sight of each other's perfection and thought of the pleasure they were about to betroth to each other.

He couldn't contain his feeling for her any longer and drew her tightly towards him as he kissed her franticly, not knowing if it would all end abruptly. First he kissed her on her lips and then worked his way down the side of her neck.

Supporting and holding her arms one by one, kissing down to the very tips of her fingers before kissing back up to her chest, still holding her hands lovingly as he kissed around her pert, hard nipples. Becoming hard himself, he ached inside with anticipation and excitement of them both becoming one. Holding her waist, he knelt down before her as he lightly open-kissed down to and then below her belly button where she held his head and stopped him from going any further. She was scared but excited all at the same time so she only stopped him briefly so she could sit down on the bed.

She sat down, perched at the edge of the bed with her knees tight together to bring herself to his eye level. He placed each hand over each of her knees and began delicately rubbing his fingers in circles before stroking up and down the sides of her legs in bigger circles gently and repetitively over and over, allowing her to part them if and when she was ready. He would never force her to do anything she didn't want to do, especially something like this. It was going to be at her pace all the way and that is why she adored him so.

His hands moved with her as she hesitantly parted her legs slightly, slowly at first, as he looked up to her one last time, reassuring her with his tender gaze that it was safe for her to trust in him and to have these feelings towards him. He leant down and kissed his way forward on the tops of her thighs as she opened her legs fully. He kissed to the top of her thigh and felt what no one else had ever felt before, the warmth of her on his lips as she laid back on to the bed and surrendered herself to him. She raised one of her legs up over his shoulder, resting it softly on his back and pulled him into her. She looked down and could see him in-between her. He delicately embraced her with his tongue but was exceptionally careful so as not to bruise or damage the delicate petals of her flower she had allowed him to be the first person to touch.

He licked and played with her as she started to experience sensations she had never felt before. Arching her back with ecstasy, feeling these emotions of desire rushing and engulfing deep inside her entire body as she let out faint groans of pleasure while grabbing at the sheet covers helplessly either side of her as she was drowned and overcome with orgasms.

He continued to suck as she orgasmed, drinking her love juice as she calmly finished. He licked her upwards one last time before showing himself to her as he stalked her body with kisses as he rose towards her, face to face. Suspended over the top of her, he hovered, gently brushing against her as he lightly placed and positioned himself at the outer edge of her flower before slowly, carefully, inserting himself inside her untouched flower, wet and tight with excitement.

They synced together in perfect motion, enjoying that the complete love, desire and passion they had held for each other for so long was now being unleashed to pleasure each other.

As he thrust himself deep towards her one final time, holding himself up against her, she could feel him pulsing inside her, leaving his gift of creamy warm milk. Once he had finished, he laid on top of her out of breath, resting from his exertion before finally withdrew from her gently and laid beside her. She turned to one side so he could spoon and relax. He held her tight and thanked her silently with an abundance of kisses all over her back and neck before relaxing further, back down into the pillow and falling into a contented tingling sleep while holding the women of his dreams securely in his arms.

That was it, it was too late for negotiations. He was so tired, so comfortable, totally overwhelmed by how he felt about this girl he had only met six months ago. Holding onto her tightly, he never wanted to let her go. She was the one, the one he wanted to spend his whole life with. As she felt the weight of his arm draped over and around her waist get heavier and become more relaxed as he drifted off to dream, she thought to herself, *he's the one, the one I want to spend my life with, make memories with, make mistakes with, make a home with, make a family with, make... make love with.* She too drifted off in the dizziness of relaxation and overwhelming tiredness. She closed her eyes and slipped into sleep, content with the choice she made. Then, suddenly...

Squark, squark, whoop, whoop, squark, squark whoop, whoop. The alarm clock made her jolt as it squawked and whooped relentless and uncaringly at them from the bedside cabinet. Without raising her head from the pillow or opening her eyes, she reached out with her free hand and blindly padded around with the hope of eventually swatting the alarm clock and turning it to snooze, wishing for another 10 minutes before having to get up. She succeeded on the fourth swat and was more than proud with her achievement. She retracted her arm, noticing his was still draped across her waist.

She turned her head towards him while raising his arm off her so she could turn onto her back. He slept heavily through the alarm; she moved and placed his arm down in front of his body. She lay there watching him while he slept silently with a faint sense of contentment as her lip raised and crinkled up on one side to reveal a half smile.

'J... J... J,' she whispered louder each time, trying to wake him from his slumber.

'Mm...' was his response, still with his eyes shut tight, more asleep than awake.

Eventually he blinked, gradually waking as he focused on her lying beside him. He took a huge breath in through his nose, held his breath as he stretched every single muscle of his body outwards like a starfish and rolled on to his back. He exhaled forcefully out as he rolled back on to his side to face her, before re-cuddled her, closing his eyes once more with no sense of urgency to get up and spoke to her with a half-awake voice. 'Good morning, gorgeous.' He turned and nuzzled back into her as he always did, reaching around her waist, playing with and linking her fingers with his. He did eventually open and focus his eyes to look into her soul once more.

She looked before turning her body round to lay and face him, mesmerized, drifting into his eyes lovingly. They were still chocolate only slightly lighter, faded around the edge now with a brushed ring of paler white chocolate circling them. As he smiled, the lines of all those years laughing became more prominent, more deeply imbedded crevices scratched across the landscape of his weathered face.

She looked down at his chest as it lightly sagged when he laid to one side. His tummy wasn't as firm as it used to be but also listed and fell to one side with a hint of "too many doughnuts consumed at work and not enough physical exercise". Wrinkled skin, crumpled memory. His hair was now receding with more salt running through it than pepper. Legs no longer running around in a frenzy but quietly and calmly, respectful of the pavement beneath them as he stepped caringly. That tall dark handsome man may have matured into a faded version of himself over the fifty years they had spent together, and time may have taken its toll and stripped him of his visual beauty, but he still possessed all the beauty within his soul. The gentleman who she had continuously loved from the first moment she saw him still existed deep inside.

Unblemished, unaltered and full of love and adoration, they indulged in a life of glorious memories and sharing precious moments throughout their entire time spent together. Changing from a boyfriend, becoming a husband, to a father, keeping strong and having endurance, continuing to be true through challenging times, together, teamwork and now the celebration of retirement and a lifelong friendship of two people whose love for each other had never faltered, still burning as strong as ever, deep inside.

'Happy anniversary, Grandar and Nanna!' erupted excitedly and squeakily from the door as it flew open. It was flung open by their three very overexcited grandchildren running in, waving a banner as they clambered on to the bed to greet them with morning kisses.

They had all had a sleepover and were now wide awake and had been for the last three hours waiting for them to wake up so they could all start the fun and games while their respective parents, J and A's handsome son and beautiful daughter with their respective partners, were busy in the kitchen, chatting and making breakfast and coffee.

True love lasts forever.

El amor verdadero dura para siempre.

6

Surrender

It was a most marvellously enjoyable and very successful afternoon that advanced late into the evening, full of fun, laughter and mindless chit-chat as he formally introduced her to his closest, most important, trusted and influential friends for the first time. They had only just started dating, officially boyfriend and girlfriend for two months now and she was keen to make a good impression. From her knowledge of all of his previous relationships, he tended to have a track record of them lasting very briefly once his friends had the opportunity and free access to analyse, pull apart, scrutinise, dissect, and finally report back to him to share their findings as to whether they thought any of them worthy to continue dating. A little bit concerning as he valued their opinions entirely.

He would undoubtedly be holding conferences and meetings with each one of them over the following week. In the office, through zoom calls and sending emails back and forth to each and every one of them. Collaborating, divulging, examining all the evidence they had gathered, explore, inspect, study, and digest all the information in order to make a final decision.

They would be brutally honest and tell him straight whether it was worth his while continuing with her. Should he remain and invest any more time, emotions or energy into a journey moving forward with her, or cut the strings now and walk away? Judge, jury and executioner come to mind, and they all had axes to hand.

The fate of their relationship lay solely in the hands of his network of friends that surrounded her today. They would ultimately decide if she was worthy of his investment and, of course, being privy to sharing or depleting many if not all of his bank accounts and of course the chalet in the alps, apartment in Gib and the little hide away in Florida Keys. They could and would make or break them.

So, she spent the entire time that day dutifully entertaining, clearing up and looking after their every need and or want. They all stood around in the garden and summer house during the day enjoying the sunshine and warmth, drinking their way through copious amounts of alcohol and eating tray after tray of nibbles and finger food all the while boasting about their yachts, houses in the south of France, bonuses, cars, and holidays. She listened and smiled politely as if she were the maid, unless they spoke or asked her probing questions about her family and their statuses.

She was so glad when the afternoon drifted leisurely into the early evening where it grew cooler with a chill in the air, before it inevitably moved forwards into the evening and night time when the firepit was lit. It gave off an inviting and mesmerising flicker of orange and intense warmth on your face from the flame. Some who were clearly more fuelled with alcohol had internal boilers burning and braved the ferocious mosquitoes outside, but the others, more faint-hearted, soft-centred or just not as drunk, gradually snuck into the conservatory, taking solace in the warmth on the sofas. They brought their life supports in from the garden with them, disguised as half empty bottles and half full glasses of champagne, pushing past her, making themselves comfortable.

She continued their ridiculous game, still checking constantly they all had full glasses, still replenishing their nibble plates, still waiting on them making sure they all had sufficient food, still emptying and clearing tables, still washing and cleaning, making sure everyone was enjoying themselves and didn't want for anything. All the while, she was, despite all that, still being judged, scrutinised, talked about, questioned, quizzed, examined, investigated, interrogated, as if she was on trial, but then again... she was. She didn't totally loathe them, she just didn't know them, and they weren't letting her into the circle just yet.

Today she was there on show and to entertain, fly the flag and socialise, doing it for him. She did it very well on queue. She never faltered, not even once, throughout the entire day. They couldn't find any cracks or chinks in her armour; she undoubtedly was the perfect host. Probably because she was the perfect match for him and they were unquestionably meant for each other. Regardless of what they were going to say about her in private conversations that would take place after the event, he adored her as did she him.

She relished playing the host in his house, pondering in her mind, considering how she would and could fit in rather respectfully on a more permanent basis. If he was to ask her, that is. Entertaining and socialising came extremely naturally to her, being a caring soul and wanting to please everyone all the time, not in a needy but a helpful, affectionate sort of way. She stood taking a breath and watched him through the open French windows from the conservatory. She observed him as he laughed out loud with no filter, just totally and completely enjoying the time with his friends. She smiled peacefully, content with how the day had unfolded, but now she just wanted everyone to leave so she could serve him privately and give him all he desired. Similarly, he wanted the reward her for her service today. He owed her one.

The time finally came as the last of the alcohol-fuelled friends staggered away, wobbling down the gravel driveway into the distant darkness, way past where the edge of the spotlights could shine. As they became consumed by the darkness, with only the remains of their slurred singing to distinguish them, he looked at her through his glassy, bloodshot eyes he had acquired from the copious amount he had drunk and gave her an unattractive, soggy kiss on her forehead before observing the empty driveway. They waved into the blind night before closing the door, switching the interior lights off and making their way up the winding stairs to bed at the end of a very lengthy and tiring day.

They undressed and freed themselves from their smoky clothes from the firepit and washed away the remains of the day in the shower. She then sat in front of the very impressive, grand dressing table, which belonged to his mother, to dry her hair and prepare to go to bed, not to relax but to have their own private entertainment and pleasure. She thought.

The games began but this evening was a little bit shorter than the usual marathon with only the basic duty of satisfaction on both parts, but enjoyable all the same. Once they gorged themselves and greedily stole pleasure from each other in abundance, they both began to wane, overwhelmed with tiredness as they had totally drained every ounce of energy from each other. Time trickled away from them steadily as they drifted off to sleep, neither of them prepared to fight any longer – tiredness had won, hands down. Quietly side by side, peacefully and securely in each other's arms, they surrender to the night. Allowing time to drive into the next morning where the sun greeted them and showed off the start of the next new day, through the opened window.

Slowly awakening, stirring from slumber, peaceful and content, she lay there looking at the vast calm white ceiling with only its heavily jewelled and sparkling ornate light hanging above her. After a night of basic reciprocal passion and pleasure, the room now stood as tranquil and peaceful as a mill pond, almost as if the room had never been touched with the only exception being the movement from the voile curtains brushing across the whitewashed wooden floor. The breath of the light breeze blew past the opened doors, through the white shutters that led out onto the Juliet balcony. The shutters were opened slightly at an angle letting delicate slices of light into the room that shone on the ornate light making it sparkle and shine spots of light throughout the entire room as she reminisced after the night full of ravenousness.

She turned her head to the side to face the open door as the birds full of song were busy chattering to each other outside as they started their day of gathering, reminding her she too was at the start a brand-new day. What would that new day bring, she wondered to herself as she turned her head back to face him. Delighted with her entertaining talents, and her private show last night, she had so many thoughts of passion and wanting to please him to the extreme. She couldn't help but start to chase her fingers through his chest hair, foraging her way to his nipples while he lay on his back still sleeping off the copious amounts of alcohol he had consumed the day and night before. She circled his nipples one way then the other as she lightly placed her leg over the outside of his, reaching her knee high, pulling his pelvis towards her, pressing up against him, drawing him closer and tighter to hers.

Running her hand down his belly, under her leg, she let her hand slip down and around his toned waist, her fingers channelling between the dips of his protruding muscles while pulling him in even closer. He began to stir slightly and rolled to face her but still had his eyes closed tightly. Closer, she reached and arched her pelvis as she firmly burrowed her fingernails into his back.

He stirred and woke sluggishly as she arched back a little to permit him access to bend forward and kiss her cleavage, if he wanted too. Firmly clasping her breast in his hand, he blindly felt his way to her awakened and pert breast, massaging and rolling her nipple between his finger and thumb, tugging it as he licked, bit and sucked at her other more exposed breast. She had woken the dragon and now, he filled his lungs, fully extending his chest out with the sweet fresh air. His heartbeat quickened with a sense of urgency, a tingling, burning desire that ran uncontrollably through his entire body to his core. His touch became unrefined and harsher as now his dragon had become even more alert to her presence and seized the moment to instigate a repeat of last night. The want and need to take his prize once more.

He rolled to lay on to his back while the pressure built and intensified inside him as he surrendered himself, giving her permission to do whatever she wanted to him. So she grabbed the opportunity to be greedy and straddled him, strategically placing herself directly on top of his groin, trapping his aching penis between them. He could feel her body weight pressing firmly down against him.

Fulfilled and content with the sensation of warmth from her covering, hiding his firm, engorged penis, he laid there enjoying every moment. She gently tilted her pelvis, rocking seductively backwards and forwards, increasingly pushing, and rubbed herself on to him, letting her lip's part further on each motion from the weight pushing down onto him, silently inviting him to feel her cushioning softness and warmth.

She felt him start to rock back and forth in time with her but more aggressive and unrefined, feeling his buttocks sharply clench and retracting, building pressure as he attempted on each motion to manoeuvre himself more, determined to enter inside, to feel her hot wet inviting pussy all around him again. With her eyes shut tightly, she leant back even further and rested her hands on his legs to intensify her fantasy and pleasure, screaming silently inside with utter excitement.

Firmly skimming his hands from her hard and aroused nipples, down both sides, he took control of and slightly adjust the location of her bottom over him, to his advantage. She felt him enter inside her swollen lips and allowing him to glide deep up inside, rubbing past her G-spot as she pushed herself down onto him fully.

With his clamps secure around her, she opened her eyes to witness his solid heavyweight biceps contracting as he positioned her. He retracted himself out of her as he lifted her off him to the tip of his shaft, before pulling her back down, impaling her as he thrust himself upwards deeper and harder, relentlessly forcing her to succumb to his strength and power. She started to feel the electrifying joy race through her body from the fierce penetration, finding ecstasy in the harsh roughness. The brutal force of his girth and length filled her to the brim with exhilaration and left her increasingly breathless.

She could feel him going deeper inside, further than anyone had ever reached. No one had thrilled her like this before. She wrenched back to intensify the sensation travelling through her entire body up through her stomach, her rib cage, only being obstructed at her throat as if she was being suffocated internally by him, asphyxiated by his power. He pulled her close, holding her onto him firmly as he positioned and twisted her around while he was still deep inside, flipping her over so she was now lying on her back with him on top, in control – the alpha male, the conqueror.

She had never been with anyone like him before, she had never felt this way about anyone.

As she let out a gasp for air, he retracted, bringing himself just to the edge of her and stopped, slightly outside but still making contact, with the rim of his head at her lips. Towering over her body at arm's length he panted as he looked at her. He paused momentarily, experiencing the sensation of slight coldness from being outside. As the moist exposure on her lips held him, he pushed forward and impaled her again and again and again relentlessly.

They were unaware of anything around them, engulfed in each other's hot sweet breath, as their searching tongues fought and tugged against each other, inhaling and exhaling each other's breath deeply. They filled their lungs, trying to keep in rhythm and control their now even more heightened eagerness as they indulged further.

She wrapped her legs around his back and locked them tightly at her ankles. With her heel grasping the back of his buttocks, she greedily puller him towards her harder and faster on each motion trying to take control and satisfy her craving of indulgence and gluttony. The pace became more frantic. He held his breath as he dug in with his toes, trying to secure his footing in the scrunched up crisp white Egyptian cotton sheet now untidily pushed and forced down to the base of the bed. Cushions and pillows littered the floor around the bed, along with discarded clothing scattered everywhere from the doorway to the bed.

Trying to concentrate on his motion, he began to increase the speed as he retracted less and the friction became more and more intense. She couldn't control it any longer and started groaning out loud with pleasure on every exhale, starting softly at first and then increasing in volume as she groaned faster and louder with the uncontrollable pleasure she was diving into and being absorbed by her own finale. She felt herself involuntarily convulsing, orgasming deep within her body, starting to shake uncontrollably, taking her away from the streamline synchronisation she had built up and nurtured as she succumbed to the hysterical overwhelming desire surging through her body.

It was his turn to be submissive to her convulsions, tightening, engorging, overpowering him as he buried himself, burrowing as deep he could inside for the final time, pinning her down while digging his fingers deep, one hand on her bum cheek, drawing her to him securely, not permitting her to escape. The other hand supported his weight while he uncontrollably pulsed inside, shooting his creaminess as far as he could up into her, leaving behind the prize, the finale, the goal they both craved.

Blissfully unaware and totally whipped up in their own pleasure, they voiced their exhaustion as they gradually slowed their erratic breathing. He released his grasp, permitting her body to relax away as he lowered his body onto hers. She could feel him still inside but relaxed now, resting, occasionally pulsing after the frantic performance. His weight was still heavy as he laid limp on top of her and restricted any movement of her body. She released and unhooked her legs from behind his back and let them lay down outside of his legs with him still erect and firmly inside her. Fluttering like butterflies with delight and satisfaction throughout her whole body, she drifted back down to reality.

They lay there, still, listening to their breath slowly easing, gradually returning to the peacefulness with his head resting over one breast so he could hear her heart pounding, fighting for its life, attempting to break through her chest. Eventually, with a gradual slowness, they resumed to normality as the birds chatted away outside.

He lifted his head, parting his body from hers like a plaster being pealed back. First he lifted his head from her breast, supporting his weight with his arms as he parted their chests and then drawing himself cautiously and slowly from inside her. She felt the sensation of him slipping out of her as he pulled himself away gradually until he was gone. She felt his absence and steadily collapsed behind him until she was completely closed with only his sticky cream left on her surrounding lips. She lay there, indulged and content.

She opened her eyes and looked up at him as he knelt over her. Looking down, he focused solely on her large green eyes glistening back at him. He smiled contentedly with a satisfying glow. Rolling to one side and laying once again in the position they had started, he closed his eyes, turned to her and muttered softly...

'Coffee, milk, no sugar.'

7

Life's a Beach

She laid there at the secluded and isolated part of the island on the comfortably cushioned four-poster double sunbed lounger at the very edge of the blinding white sandy beach. She had positioned herself in a prime location sheltered underneath the bowed, outstretched umbrella palm trees. They extended out over the shallows as the slowly lapping ocean repeatedly jumped forward and rippled back over the purest fine grains of sand attempting to lure them, drag them back calmly into the sea.

The sunbed was heavily ladened and surrounded at the sides and back by pure white organza, swathed across the frame in abundance.

Layer upon layer, some stretched whereas others were partly secured and then fell freely and hung over each of the sides. The top was stretched taut above her between the frame as a canopy, sheltering her from the relentless rays and halting the tiny grains of sand from penetrating through the fabric and reaching her. The loose fabric gently swayed back and forth, dancing from the warm comforting breath of the tropical breeze as it occasionally strolling past.

Tiresomely, the grains persistently attempted to slink through its multiple layers of security barriers to steal a touch or lick of her exposed, toned, tight, tanned body. But they were all deflected and flicked to the floor where they collected and made miniature sand dunes all around her.

The layers obscured and put a stop to any prying eyes from annoying swimmers trying to catch a prohibited glimpse as they casually swam by, past the small coves and rocks at the side of the bay that separated them from the more densely populated public beach to the side of them. Looking out to sea, it was hard to distinguish where the ocean stopped and the sky started as it merged together in a faint hazy blur of darker shades as it stretched into the distance.

The ocean was a spectrum of blues painted in front of her on a canvas, created by nature which seemed to have been painted especially for her. It ranged from crystal clear water at her feet with brushstrokes of aqua and sapphire, and moved further away to a bottomless pacific blue. The colours merged, immersed and embellished into one another harmoniously, as the currents swirled and collided them all together. The few wisps of white clouds overhead leisurely glided across the sky, only to be evaporated from existence, made extinct by the intense heat of the day, never to reach their destination.

She was scantily dressed, relaxed in a very revealing, minuscule red bikini. A high-cut leg with gold buckles that clasped each side, almost at her waist, a plunging bra with delicate shoestring straps, also with a matching buckle clasp at the centre, just under her cleavage. Her body was so toned it was as if she was a moving bronze statue.

Stomach muscles so firm, she sat up effortlessly and raised her hand to shield her eyes from the intense brightness as she searched far out to sea, skimming across the horizon. *Where is he, where has he gone?* she thought to herself. Then, she saw him, the small object of her desire, a dot on the horizon interrupting the calm flat stillness of the water. There he was on the surface, swimming closer. She partly relaxing back down and rested on one elbow as she adjusted her other hand over her forehead so she could continue to watch him as he approached closer with a satisfactory smile. Eventually he reached a point where he was no longer able to swim and made the transition, became upright and started to walk through the shallows to the shore. The top of his body slowly emerged from the bath of warm salty water, exposing *his* bronzed, toned, perfectly formed and pumped body. Breaking free from the depths, the surface water desperately tried to cling to him, requesting him to stay, as it lapped softly and delicately at his waist.

The ocean could no longer ensnare his now upright body, so it began to cascade and fall down his rippling muscles as they contracted as he continued walking forcefully with conviction through the water. It eventually but reluctantly let him go. As he gradually pushed forward, the water wrapped itself around his engorged thigh muscles, encouraging them to stay as he worked them, cutting through, and getting closer to the shoreline. As he trekked forward, the depth of the water lessened, and walking became easier as he escaped from its grasp. He was released and exposing more and more of himself to her, especially what his drenched trunks where clinging on too. The fabric was being overprotective but, in reality, showcasing his rather well-endowed special package rather exceptionally, as if it was being personally delivered for her approval.

Is that all for me? she thought to herself as she unknowingly bit her lower lip with excitement and anticipation as her eyes widened and the fluttering activated inside just from him being close to her.

Out of the painting he steadily walked surefooted towards her, escaping the sea's hold. She watched him silently with only the sound of the water droplets lazily falling casually as they followed him out of the sea. Once he was free, the salty warm water began to skate down the crevices and curves of his physique and fell helplessly to the ground being absorbed by the dry, thirsty sands. Now he was totally uncovered, he couldn't hide. His nipples became hard as bullets as the breeze gently licked past them. His trunks surrendered their possessive grasp as he moved on land with the sea water relaxing, giving in to gravity as droplets fringed the hem of each leg of his trunks.

He walked towards her, flicking and kicking up dust particles from the sand caught in his toes with every footstep. He was captivated by her beckoning look and seductive smile. She lowered her hand from her forehead as the need to shield her eye was no longer necessary as he reached the base of the lounger and stood towering over her with the sun now hiding behind his silhouette.

He crouched down, took both her feet securely in his hands before kissing her immaculately manicured toes, giving her goosebumps from the contact with the coolness of his body touching hers. She laid there satisfied, revelling in the attention. She tolerated the chill and let him continue now he had rejoined her from his morning swim.

Captivated, he padded with his lips travelling up over her feet, then her legs, giving her free kisses at close intervals as he hovered, elevated, moving up above her. Parting her legs with his hands at her knees, he shifted his attention and bigger longer kisses to her inner thighs, continuing up to her bikini bottoms at her pelvis where he paused and lightly nuzzled and caressed her with the tip of his nose. He seized the moment and enjoyed the control, creating an atmosphere of anticipation, heightening the intense yearning she was already experiencing. He was aware that the dull fluttering ache strengthened and pulled at her from inside her pelvis contracted, underneath the calm facade. She made her feelings known vocally and sighed as she willingly parted her legs even more as she succumbed to his touch.

Now enticed by his enchantment, he continued to the top of her bikini bottoms, stroking his nose across her soft velvet toned body, closely followed by more free kisses before reaching her belly button. It was waterlogged and drowning from its pool of resting salty water, gently carried and deposited there by the droplets that fell from his sea-drenched hair. As he kissed down on her indented belly, the water expelled, cascading down each side of her, blotting and disappearing into the plush towel she was resting on.

Now with moistened lips, he continues his adventure, kissing his way up the centre of her body, in between her mountainous cleavage held securely in place by the clasp and buckle. He continued up through her chest, around her neck, leaving delicate little prints of moist lip marks behind him which quickly evaporated with the heat. He finally reached the finish line, her beautifully, warm and inviting pert lips brushed with gloss. The warmth of her body and the coldness of his collided like opposites spectrums of temperatures, fighting each other at first for survival, but eventually subsiding being submissive to each other's presents, happily uniting, finding a middle ground as he lowered his body unhurriedly onto hers.

Brushing her legs across the lounger they found their way to circle around his buttocks so she could feel his wet trunks and the contents, cold and hard at her pelvis. She pushed up against him while his weight and gravity pushing down to join her. With her arms and legs wrapped firmly around him and lips locked in a kiss, he threaded one arm between the towel and her back, supported himself as well as her weight and scooped her up clear off the bed and suspended her in his arms in the middle of the sun lounger holding her firmly in front of him. Securely in his arms, he hauled and elevated them up vertically before moving his legs around to sit his bottom on the lounger while she was still suspended in front of him. Slowly he released his grip, and with the help of gravity, she started to fall, gradually being lowered into his lap.

She was totally aware of him completely erect, underneath her, waiting for her slightly parted lips to fall down onto him. With her legs wrapped around his waist, it made her more exposed and impeccably positioned. She deliberately loosened the grip of her legs so they too dropped and relaxed onto the soft cushioned lounger just behind him but still touching his bottom with her heels. He felt her loosen her grip so held her bottom and took the weight of her body and held her there, suspended just above the tip of his firm, blood-engorged penis, letting it taste and brush her open lips delicately, teasing her through her bikini.

Her fingers combed through his sea-drenched hair as she kissed him vigorous and generously all over his face, losing herself in the whirlwind that started to whip around and encase them both. He lowered her down into his lap so his hands were free to wander, discovering the clasps at each side of her bikini bottoms. Without sight, he cleverly touched and worked out the mechanics to effortlessly unfastened the buckle with one hand while his other distracted her attention by caressing her breast. The tautness of her bikini bottoms slackened when the buckle became loosened; she knew what he was doing and was more than happy for him to continue, not acknowledging the act but growing hornier with the knowledge it would soon be time for the next performance. Her only concern was if he would be as efficient when unbuckling the other side to free her and expose her to him. She felt the fabric disappear from her body. Oh, she thought gladly, he was. It was done. He held onto the back of the now draped, lifeless bikini bottoms and politely pulled them through her legs and away from her bottom before tossing them to one side of the lounger.

She bent her legs and brought them to each side of him, so as to kneel with him between her legs. She supported her own weight now, to make a small space between them. Leaning back slightly with his legs out straight in front of him, he raised his pelvis and brushed against her uncovered lips as he attempted to pull down and free himself from his damp, sea-riddled trunks by wriggling from bum cheek to bum cheek in the gap between them. Tugging down at the waist, he wriggled out of them unrefined and clumsily. Once they were past his bottom he could manoeuvre them with his legs, down to his ankles, where he kicked them clean away before sitting back upright to join her again to continue with the performance.

As she knelt over him, a leg each side, her breasts at eye level, he looked down and saw her, shaved and smooth, just waiting for the entertainment to start. She too took a sneaky glance down between her legs to see him there, strong and fully erect, waiting for her to lower herself down on top of him. She peacefully positioned herself over him, lowering and edging herself towards him, slowly while crouching and leaning forward slightly to allow her lips to spread further naturally. As her lips kissed his freezing firmness with her warmth and invitingness, its chill rushed through her body before it settled and lured him in. She could feel his cold skin on her hot wet opening as she lowered and edged herself down further onto him, just enough for him to enter inside her house of pleasure. Enjoying the sharpness and firmness of his ice as it entered her, she felt his presence from her lips deep into her core, warming his coldness as he travelled deeper.

Edging herself even further down, pushing into him, greedily pleasuring her hunger, she could feel him moving up inside, as she fully sat down on to his lap and grated forward, attempting to eat more. She paused there just for a moment and clenched herself as she could feel his groin kiss her inner lips, knowing she had completely consumed him. Still clenched, she gently raised herself, tilted her hips out towards her bottom and allowed him to escape her slightly, before harshly thrusting forward and swallowing him once more, letting their groins join together and savagely kissing him again.

Rocking and tilting backwards and forwards, she could feel the girth of him rubbing between her lips, over her clit, pushing up against her cervix deep as she steadied and secured herself by placing both her hands on his shoulders and imbedding her fingers into his tanned skin.

With both his hands glued to her buttocks, he steadily pulling her back onto him after every stroke she took. She raised and dropped herself, continuing to massage and rub him from inside. Faster and faster, until the soft rock and tilt became a shoving, ferocious and aggressive thrusting, back and forth, repetitively, like the piston of an out-of-control steam train heading for a crash. Until suddenly, without any warning, he held her captive and strongly, squeezing her bottom onto him, not allowing her to withdraw or retract from him anymore.

With the abrupt halt to the motion, she could feel him inside, pulsating his creamy offerings into her while all she could hear was her heart pounding in her head. She seized him, buried inside. They sat there descending from the climax, catching their breath and returning to earth as she clenched around him still inside her, enjoying his girth against her walls of velvetiness. Sitting on top of him, in each other's arms, not wanting to pull apart, wanting to make the moment last longer. They enjoyed the excitement and contemporariness of their connection and remembered how they both rejoiced in sex alfresco.

Now calm was beginning to be restored, she pulled herself away from him, reaching fully and stretching over to the side of him to claim an opened bottle of Champaign lying to the side of the lounger and rescued it from the ice bath it was swimming in. Grasping it at its neck she retrieved and rescued it from the chill of the ice bucket. She glugged its contents into the two glasses he was holding, before replacing the bottle back into the ice to rest. With glass in hand, they relaxed back on to the lounger side by side to refocus on the picture before them out to sea.

The arrangements and variations of beautiful blue swirls that immersed into one another were still there, but had now been savagely interrupted. They gasped and watched with horror as someone had indignantly, without permission, painted an enormous overpowering 12-deck cruise liner ship in the middle of their painting.

The ocean liner's occupant's, passengers and staff were lined up, staring at them open-mouthed, grasped in horror at the sight they had just witnessed, thinking, *This wasn't on the itinerary.* Others clapped and applauded with adoration and disbelief at the amazing show they had been privileged to be a part of.

Now totally aware of the sound of distant cameras clicking, that would develop the evidence, phones held high, lazily videoing to document the show to share with their particular group chats, they also heard and concentrated on the applause and wolf whistles from others. All they could do was turn to each other clink glasses, raise them to the spectators, take a sip and giggle together.

They got up off the lounger to gather up and collect the clothes they had scattered and abandoned, held them in bundles close to themselves, casually attempting to cover up as modestly as they could. With no guilt they unashamedly retreated, walking casually back to the patio of the beach house they were renting. They passed through the door before turning round and bowing one last time to the audience before closing the door behind them to play out the rest of the day in privacy.

They had undoubtedly just had a busy and energetic afternoon in the unexpected spotlight. No wonder the beach houses were at a reduced rate.

8

On your Knees

She was overjoyed and relieved to finally be home after the usual, uneventful, unenthusiastic uninspiring visit to the local supermarket to get a few bits she had forgotten to include with her online shopping that week. We all know a "few bits" means spending three times more money than you originally anticipated. Not taking enough bags means that the contents spill out over the top because you've crammed everything in and it's so heavy, with handles screaming from strain, ready and poised to break at any given second.

She struggled through the lounge, avoiding the obstacle course of rubbish and debris littering the floor and coffee table left there by the offspring following the mass exodus to feed their every increasing appetite for socialising. She eventually reached the kitchen, exhausted. Her arms were loaded with the overbearing weight of the heavy bags of shopping, fingertips turning purple from the lack of blood supply because the flow had been cut off from holding the hefty cargo. Eventually, as she reached the kitchen, she was nearing the finish line as she approached and went up on her tiptoes, lifting the bags together, hoisting then up and discharging them both onto the counter. She gave out a sigh in pure relief as she tentatively unthreaded her fingers out of the handles of the shopping bags. Her hands now free but she was still unable to uncoil them straight, contorted as they were from the torture of clutching the bags for such a long time.

While she took a moment massaging and rubbing her hands and fingers encouraging them to regain consciousness, she pondered on where to deposit and stow away the food she'd just unnecessarily brought home. Opening the already full top cupboards, she rearranged the contents to allow the new arrivals to sit proud next to the other boxes and packets. She moved onto the glass jars and tins now, taking them out as she bent down before she completely knelt down onto the kitchen floor on her knees to rummage to the far depths of the bottom cupboard in the darkness, foraging to feel for the tins to organise and make space for the new arrivals. The fresh delivery needed to be placed carefully in the bottom cupboard so if they fell out, they wouldn't fall far. She was a stickler for safety as a tin had fallen out on her feet previously and she didn't relish it happening again.

While she was bending over, preoccupied, she was made aware of him being there as his leg brush up firmly and stroked the outside of her thigh as he leant over her to switch the kettle on. He had been on nights that week and had just woken up weary when he heard her come in noisily with the bags. He was more than happy to be woken as it was four o'clock in the afternoon and he had to be back in work again by seven. So it gave him time to shower, get sorted and engage in general chit chat of how her day had been before he had to leave. But something else had awoken from its slumber and stayed burning deep inside of him with an overwhelming urge that he needed to extinguish first.

He knelt down behind her and rested there, snuggling close to her bum, spooning and rubbing himself up against her. He wrapped his arm around and underneath her belly and cuddled her waist as he leant forward over her back. Peacefully he paused for a moment, nestling into her radiating warmth.

His friend started to wake up too, wearily at first but then growing stronger and wrestled to free itself through his lounger trousers generating tension at the front and pressing firmly against her skirt. He shifted his hands gradually and slowly from her waist and felt around unhurriedly from the hem of her skirt up her thigh to her hip, in search of her thong. His fingers glided up her smooth soft thigh and his fingertips came in contact with the lace trim. He threaded his fingers around, caught hold of the side and with no sense of urgency started to free her of the burden, releasing her and coercing her to relinquish herself to his desires. He held firmly and guided the thong down her thighs where they rested on the floor, captured by her slightly parted legs at her knees. She knelt there, submissive, because she wanted it just as much as he did. He began to raise up her skirt so he could look at and fully expose her peach bottom.

He lent back to admire the exhibit in front of him, running his fingertips over and caressing his hands around each cheek, he inspected every inch. Carefully he pulled forward and hooked his lounger trousers waistband over and down past his outstretched erect friend to release him from the darkness into the light because he was ready for action after lying dormant all day. He lingered for a moment, placing one hand on the base of her back and the other around his friend to start to manoeuvre, pushing his pelvis closer to her, guiding himself manually into pole position at the opening of her lips. Feeding time at last. He placed himself at her lips and firmly but gradually pushed himself inside her in one continuous force. Feeling every inch being swallowed, once he had established himself fully, he moved both hands to her sides and closed his eyes to fill his mind with the ecstasy and pleasure of being in her fully. As the motion took hold he stabilised and supported their bodies then returned to his fantasy and emporium, his own secluded and private paradise in his mind.

With heightened arousal tinkling after a while, he opened his eyes, returning to watching himself disappearing into her lips, in and out repetitively from behind her. He watched them wrapping themselves around him as he moved in-between them, deep into her warm, sticky pussy. Back and forth, disappearing into the darkness of pleasure and out, only to be pushed back in again harder and faster the next time. She gripped his foreskin so very tightly when he entered deep each time, pushing it back, rubbing the inside of her hot wet pussy all over as it surrounded and engulfed his hard engorged nakedness as she allowed him to glide in and out gracefully.

Holding each side of her at her hips, maintaining a firm grip, he could guide himself into her accurately on each thrust while stroking her lower back just above her dimples with his exposed thumbs, feeling her soft silky skin, delicate and fair, while holding her securely with his fingers wrapped around her front.

Pushing against her bum cheeks as he entered, she arched her back slightly, making an effort to push herself back onto him more, deliberately impaling herself harder on to his enormous cock, greeting him with the yearning desire to feel him even deeper insider her. Arching her back, naturally exposed her entire bum to him. She enticed and lured him in, knowing he loved to watch it pulsate and retract as he penetrated her from behind.

Seeing this as he briefly looked down, he inevitably loosened the grip of one hand to place it on the centre of her back, covering her dimples at the base of her spine. He spread out his hand like a starfish, fingers in front, he guided his thumb, angling it downwards, gently rubbing and gliding it, travelling down to her increasingly parted bum hole where the skin was darker and slightly ruched, pulled into a centre point disappearing inside her.

He reached the pinnacle, and she could feel the slightest of pressure he applied with his thumb assertively down onto her, trying to gain access inside her bum. He tilted his thumb and applied slightly more pressure as she relaxed her muscles allowing just the tip of his thumb to enter and peep inside to stretch and arouse her. He manipulated and stirred his thumb in circles, stimulating her more as he watched her swallow his thumb deeper. She felt the erotic contractions and squeezed tighter round him. Deeper and deeper she could feel the pleasurable drag of the outer skin being pulled into her from his unlubricated thumb.

He could feel himself rubbing up and down inside her against the back of his thumb through her delicate skin that separated her bum from her pussy. As he pulled himself in and out, he started to pull his thumb in and out in sync, faster and faster every time as she convulsed, contracted and tightened around both the penetrations letting out groans of ecstasy, unable to control her body while he played out his pleasure.

She wanted to part her legs to angle and eat him more but couldn't as they were snagged and restricted by her thong. She held onto and clawed at the lower shelf, thrusting herself back against him violently, frustrated because she wanted to get him even deeper inside her. Now with his thumb pushed in securely he began circling and flicking it inside her for added pleasure. She loved the double penetration and unleashed the sensations that controlled her body so she could come with multiple orgasms.

He released his grip with his other hand and held the back of her head, grabbing at her hair, holding it in his clenched fist, pulling her head back towards him making her raise her hands and placing them higher on the work surface. This created a different angle inside her again, pushing stronger against her G-spot, increasing the intensity further.

He rode her like a crazy horse, untamed, unrefined, holding onto her hair like a mane as if he was breaking her in, stamping his authority on her. He lost control as he pulsated with all his strength, brandishing her, leaving the mark of his creaminess inside her. Both were lost in the heat of the moment.

Ding dong!

After leaving his mark, he uncultured and brashly retracted both himself and his thumb and looked over his shoulder, not knowing what he expected to see behind him as the doorbell rang out once more. He rose to his feet hastily then, after pausing for a second, he swiftly grasped and tugged for the waist of his loungers. He winched and wrenched them up over his still very erect cock and secured them vigorously and hurriedly the best he could while securing his footing. He walked out of the kitchen hastily and light-headed, drained of energy from his activities, through the lounge where he stumbled and accidently kicked over a half empty cup of coffee abandoned at the corner of the sofa. Rebalancing, he composed himself the best he could before opening the front door.

'Hello,' a chirpy voice exploded from the short man standing in front of him with dark thick-rimmed glasses and a baseball cap on backwards. Arching his neck to one side, he announced, 'Shopping delivery, the lady of the house normally asks me to take it round the back for her but the gate's shut!'

As he spoke the delivery driver's eyes dropped and gazed astonishingly down towards his crotch to witness he was still very much erect, tugging and stretching his trouser fabric. He saw the driver look down and so too followed his eyes down to see what was taking his attention away.

Completely embarrassed, the driver looked back at him before averted his eyes to the side and said sheepishly and as quickly as possible so as to get the hell out of there, 'I'll just leave it here this week then, shall I? Sign here please.' He looked away while coarsely thrusting the delivery pad and pen towards him for his signature. He eagerly snatched back the pad as soon as he put the full stop at the end of his signature. Before he could say thank you, as quick as a flash, he was gone down the driveway and into the delivery van, locked the doors and sped down the road out of sight in a flash.

He closed the door more leisurely than he opened it, looked down at himself still semi-erect and thought with a smile on his face, *what a way to start my day and I'm so very gratefully the back door wasn't open today.*

9

Little Princess

Brushing her hair away flippantly with the back of her hand, she glanced back over her shoulder as she reached over casually with her other hand to flick the light switch off, walking out the door before finally tugging it closed behind her as she left the flat. She stood on the other side of it for a moment and began pawing through her bag just to check everything was correct and present before she focused her attention on getting down the stairs without breaking her neck or a leg with her 4-inch-high heels she was wearing. They looked amazing in the catalogue, and on, but actually having the ability to walk in them couldn't have been farther from the truth.

She began to think it may have been a bit of a mistake putting them on straight away rather than waiting until she was downstairs. She could have sensibly and safely fiddled and faffed with the straps and put them on whilst comfortably sitting on the plush green velvet sofa in the lobby. But that would have been too simple and straightforward for her. So she held the handrail firmly for dear life and glided her hands down in intervals, stopping and starting, gripping and releasing when she required extra support, holding on securely while she took each footstep tentatively, over barrenly on each step. Feet slightly angled to one side to where she was holding on to the rail, she took it considerably slower to get down the stairs than she normally would when wearing her ballerina pumps. With those it was a piece of cake, skipping carelessly when she was off to work, but this was the weekend, Friday night, totally different scenario.

Anyone who's anyone would tell you it's incredible tricky and near on impossible to descend steadily and in one piece down one flight of stairs, let alone three flights, wearing ridiculously towering heels. Especially after sinking countless shots of single malt whisky while getting ready to go out. That only makes it even more of a treacherous challenge that many lightweights wouldn't be able to manage.

She looked immaculate as always. On the bottom, strappy black patent skyscraper strappy shoes showing off her scarlet manicured toes, slowly working up to her mid-thigh black leather miniskirt just finishing past her bum cheeks, heaving and stretched tightly over her thighs. This was teamed with her favourite black satin strapless basque with a delicate lace trim standing to attention over her breasts that oozed out over the top. It showcased her tiny waist and her plump full breasts, forcing them up so high they were almost diving over the top for freedom but slightly hidden by a small bolero crushed velvet, short-sleeved jacket. A diamante choker and bracelet accessorised her body to finish off the outfit while her refined smooth, shiny cascading bouncing curls framed her flawless, youthful, painted face.

Finally descending and reaching the bottom of the last flight of break-your-neck stairs, she abandoned the handrail dismissively, as if she could have made it without its help all by herself attitude. Now for the next challenge of walking across the highly polished marbled lobby floor which she took with great mindfulness and diligence, with each forward step. If she was to lose her footing even just the once, it would be so undignified and embarrassing even though no one was there to be a witness to it. She would know and that was all that mattered. Concentrating, she placed each foot securely and ever so cautiously in front of the other, not just setting down her heel, but anchoring her entire foot to the floor so as not to slip, skid, or slide as she made her way to the main entrance door. She grabbed hold of the handle, pleased with herself for achieving the next phase of her evening. *It's the little things that matter,* she thought to herself. But I do believe that half a bottle of whisky chasers didn't help and marginally affected and contributed to her over all ability and judgment to choose suitable footwear.

Rotating the protruding metal latch with one hand, she repetitively nudged the stubbornly heavy steel and glass door open with her other hand and shoulder before managing to wedge it open just enough so she could squeeze through and escape into the night. Once through she let it go and listened to it creak as it very labouringly, resumed its closed position, finally clunking the latch shut behind her.

There was a distinctive variation of temperature once she had exited the building and was standing outside in the night. She had been lulled into a false sense of security inside the apartment where it was a warm, inviting and safe, away from the unfriendly slash of a chilling 11pm autumn evening. The temperature had now plummeted, and she was exposed. Her breath was a plume and could be seen clearly as she exhaled. The faint wind bit and circled around her smooth tanned arms and legs laid bare and exposed her to the frightening, hostile, iciness, giving her goosebumps everywhere it touched. The whisky warmed her slightly as she polished her arms vigorously to generate some warmth from the friction but was unsuccessful.

She ventured out into the night, not knowing what would be in store. She was eager to find out what adventures were on offer, who she would meet, and what time would she eventually get home. Who cared. An overly excited, enthusiastic, but tipsy, rocking chick sauntered on tiptoes to the club which was only a stone's throw away to meet with her usual cluster of drinking and dancing buddies. She was ready to play and experience whatever treasures the night had in store for her to discover, like a Pandora's box waiting to be opened.

Her perfume trailed in the air behind her as she sashayed along, taking notice of everyone she passed, intrigued to know if they were observing her. She made sure to be aware of any additional attention from any bystanders. Turning the corner, she could see her crew standing outside, queuing almost at the entrance. She broke into a smile and her face lit up with anticipation as she quickened her pace in eagerness to join them.

Sure-footed now she was on level ground, she began to wave at a few girls who saw her approaching and returned the gesture, greeting her with open smiles and enthusiastic waves from afar. She received these gracefully before embarking on the usual ceremonious kisses and hugs, complimenting each other on their exquisite taste and choice of attire that evening and, of course, hair and makeup.

She took her time and diligently acknowledge everyone before finding the handrail to ascend the steps. They reached the top where they paused, greeted by the towering pillars in blue bomber jackets with IDs strapped to their impressive arms. Their wide promiscuous smiles eyed the girls up and down as they casually unhooked the podium rope, holding it aloft so they could pass through, automatically permitting them access to the foyer and then re-hooking it once the last one was through. From here they could see through the glass panels of the secondary internal doors into the darkness, with occasional lights flickering and flashing at the heart of the club where the main dancefloor waited for them to play and show off. They felt the base booming and reverberating into the depth of their souls. Hearing the familiar music, they began to tap their toes, wriggle a hip and sway casually but not fully committing to the beat just yet.

Once the tariffs were paid at the booth they continued through the doors where the music became more intense, overpowering, inviting them in as they walked towards the wall of noise and light shows. Footsteps became synchronised with the beat, bodies seized and consumed, being engulfed by the atmosphere. Encapsulated by the intensity of the music, with its overwhelming loudness pulsing through their bodies, they endured the blinding lights while their eyes attempting to adjust to the surrounding darkness.

The satisfying frenzy of familiar aromas were craving to be smelt. Alcohol and aftershave were being absorbed hurriedly through their senses. The touch of carpet, cushioning beneath her feet was welcoming after walking in from the hard, cold pavement and steps outside. Everyone was in and accounted for, so they made their way through the scattering of people to find a space at the bar. Observing who had been served and was about to pay, they jostled their way forward and stood just behind the first row of people standing at the bar, ready to pounce and occupy the space when those ahead picked up their glasses and walked away. She was quite a formidable character, and all the staff knew her, so the chance she would be the one noticed and served first was pretty good. The handsome barman acknowledged her from afar as he took payment from his customer and joined her immediately as he finished. She placed the order on her tab and as soon as her drink was made, told the girls she was going to find somewhere for them all to sit. With her drink in hand, she turned and started to walk away from the bar to explore. She found a spot where she and her friends could survey all the fine talent, eye them up and down, absorb and decide who to talk to and who to deflect.

The club was a mix of chambers and coves with walkways and staircases, a labyrinth of tunnels between them, catering for everyone's tastes. Some were carpeted with lush, velvet upholstery, teamed with chaise longues, full-length arched windows draped with heavy jacquard curtains, low tables with waiter service. Seductive low-level lighting gave the illusion of it being more intimate and private than it actually was. Others had high tables, either to stand at or perch on upright stools with cushions on seats and backs. There were quiet areas where you could be more alone, chat quite comfortably, but she wanted to get intimately close and feel the heat, desire and want of another body next to hers with the tribal instinct to dance and be free of the imprisonment and restrictions of the day.

Wherever you wandered to in the club and stopped for a while, you were guaranteed to be met with quality. The venue was exquisite and spanned over all three floors, complete with balconies to look over the main dancefloor that was cradled in the lower level. It was the heart or, as some would call it, the pit of your stomach, where the music vibrated violently as the dancing continued throughout the night, never fading or ceasing. Down there you were blinded by the bright arrangement of multicoloured lighting systems changing, moving, flashing, strobing, and flickering to the thud of the base tones that would be pumped from speakers strategically arranged around a communal sea of individuals in harmony. No one talked as you would never be heard, only moving, swaying, pulsing of bodies zombified by the trancing of melody, synchronised in time with the music, being enchanted and transfixed. The dancing intensified and spilled out off the main dancefloor and over the edges out to the immediate areas as the night drew on, where more alcohol was absorbed and consumed by more people, captivated, joining the sea of faces swirling on the floor.

The girls all joined her once they had their drinks and collectively watched the performances of dancing and chatting of everyone around them, while happily standing in each other's company warming up before taking the plunge and joining in.

Hungry for attention, she scrutinized and inspected everyone who was either standing or walking by her. She decided to head off for a wander, to do a circuit of each level, slowly sieving her way through the oncoming crowds. They too were watching the exhibits, gazing and inspecting everyone, absorbing their attire, stature, posture. They were all looking at each other as potential prey, vibrant and ready to pounce if it looked intriguing enough.

Beginning to feel a little despondent and disappointed with the lack of talent from what was usually on offer, she was just about to return and regroup with the girls to see if they had any luck, when she walked on a little bit further. Then she saw him moving effortlessly towards her, a potential entertainment for the evening, possibly more, who knew. Their eyes fixed onto each other as they approached casually and confidently. She tried to look away but was drawn back in by his magnetic pull which she was unable to resist. The desire to quench her thirst for play, she couldn't control the power of his attraction, she buckled and walked straight towards him, undoubtably heading for a collision.

With both of them transfixed, she smiled to show her interest, her desire to play. He served it back to show her his acceptance of the game and confidently but casually held out his hand as he approached her, hoping to take hold of her arm. She deliberately walked closer and brushed past, colliding with him gracefully. He closed his grasp and successfully snared her, accomplishing it smoothly and with graceful confidence.

They now stood close, side by side, and she turned and stared up into his eyes and raised one eyebrow to insinuate her awareness of him catching her and thought, *Jackpot*. He too looked down at her from his towering hight with his dark wisping curls falling and resting on his defined cheek bones. He smiled widely as if he had just struck gold.

'And what's your name?' he enquired with a strong tone.

'Anastasia, and yours?'

'Harrison,' he replied.

And so it began...

The night span out of control and the club steadily filled to its capacity, which they paid no real attention to but happily tolerated the other people, only concentrating on each other. They had no choice but to move closer as others brushed past everyone else on the narrow walkways because of the increasing volume of people congregating. She enjoyed the contact as his body touched hers, gently being pressed closer together, while others passed by like grains of sand hustling to get through the narrowing gap of a timer. Before long they were so close their entire bodies were touching. She absorbed the heat of his breath on her neck as he spoke close to her ear so he could be heard. She could smell his aftershave, breathing and consuming it in like a drug, getting high from his presence.

Familiar songs played as they began to grind, harmonizing to the beat, and occasionally mouthing and singing along. Drawing her waist close while dancing, she felt his erect penis stroking and being pressed up close against her. They stood there motionless for a second as if someone had pressed the pause button. He gazed and melted into her eyes, glanced at her lips then back to her eyes as he moved closer to her, nose to nose, thighs to thighs, poised, breathing each other's breath in and out through each other's slightly opened mouths. The noise melted away, as did all the immediate people, evaporating out of focus as they began to taste each other's lips, soft at first but becoming harder, greedily reaching with their tongues, searching inside, tasting. Twisting and summersaulting, contorting, constricting, wrestling for supremacy around each other's open and inviting mouths, they were pleasantly saturated by alcohol; hers whisky, his vodka shots with a larger chaser.

Aroused and feeling the fluttering pressure mounting between her legs and the ache of her groin, she wanted him right there, right now. Impulsively, she clasped his hand so tightly her knuckles turned white. Fearing he may escape, she led the way through the crowds, holding on tight so he wouldn't be lost, glancing back occasionally just to check and reassure herself he was still there, as if her hand may have tried to deceive her in some way. The ocean of people where not making it easy for her as she fought through the strengthening current to get to a quiet, more secluded area of the club.

She knew exactly where she would take him but had to clear it first with one of the bar men she knew was working tonight, and he was on the third floor. She led him to the bar in the VIP lounge where she made eye contact with James, the smartly dressed barman, and beckoned him over. Leaning forwards to secretly speak with him, all the while still holding Harrison's hand, she could feel him pressing close up behind her, running the fingers of his free hand round her thigh, investigating the hem of her skirt. He doodled and then grasped round to her front while she was bending over, taking a keycard from the barman. When finished, she spun round to face him then continued on her quest and led him back through the increasing sea of bodies, across the corridor towards a locked door. She swiped the card turned the latch, opened it and drew him through the doorway.

They walked down a dark, narrow corridor to the end, away from the noise and nosy spectators. The club became increasingly muffled and almost muted as she turned the handle of yet another door. They were now at the very back of the club in a secluded storeroom of unused chairs and stacked boxes full of obscurities the club weren't using now.

She came to a standstill in front of one of the emerald green velvet chesterfield chairs, turned and abruptly started to kiss him repetitively on his full, welcoming lips, rudely and uninvited. Working her way down the side of his neck, he joined the party. Now with both hands free he concentrated on hitching up her skirt to her waist, revealing her thong. He sunk his hand down her front, in between her legs, dragged the crotch of her thong to one side exposing her wet, aching lips, before he lowered himself down to sit on the chair. Provocatively, she raised and kicked her leg over his lap as if she was straddling a motorbike and stood there still and silent.

He stretched her G-string further over with his thumb so he could see her fully. Her freshly shaved and smooth hood was ready for him to play with, which he did spectacularly. He leant forward into her and started to kiss her smooth front at the top before moving down, licking just underneath her front from the bottom of her hood to the top.

She stood still, enjoying the attention from his warm lips, allowing him to kiss and lick as he guided and rubbed his wandering fingers back and forth gently from her clit back to her slightly parted lips. Hooking his middle finger, he pressed and teased her lips open more and ventured inside of her, up inside her further on every repeated visit. Then he introduced his second finger to join in with the performance for her ultimate entertainment, pleasuring her further with more girth. She was enjoying his touch. She threaded her fingers through his mass of curls, pulled his head towards her, revelling with the pleasure he was giving her, feeling the increased gliding and lubrication of his fingers running around in circles inside her. She could feel his two fingers dancing deep inside with her love juice, lingering inside for longer, reaching up and twisting before retracting them while licking her front, creating a frensy of lubricated chaos.

Pulling away slightly, allowing his fingers to still be inside of her, she leant forwards to release him from the confines of his trousers and out into the cool air. He retracted his fingers from inside her and held one lip and the thong over to one side and her other lip to the other side out of the way and opened her fulling for her to eat him. Returning upright, she positioned herself over the top of him, lowered her frenzied, stimulated and lubricated pussy down on top of his vertically poised penis, swallowing him in one downward stroke, capturing him inside her. As he held her lips clear, there was no obstructions for him to deal with so he just let her sit down on his lap fully. Straight inside her, only stopping when her cushioned lips of her straddle legs lowered and kissed his lap. She watched the ecstasy erupt over his face as he reached as far as he could inside her. She kissed and licked his lips, ran her fingers back and forth vigorously through his beautifully thick curls, while raising and lowering herself on and off of him. He felt himself being pulled into and out of her as she repetitively sat down on him, filled herself completely to the brim, the entire length of him rubbing up and down inside, over and over again. Pivoting backwards and forwards, she drew him in and out at different angles, in and out of her warm inviting pussy, rubbing her clit up and down his shaft as she greedily ate him time after time.

He leant back on the chair and accepted her dominance, absorbing all of the pleasure she was bringing to his playground, before reaching around to her bum cheeks placing all fingers in between and parting them slightly to expose her bottom. He began to explore again with his fingers and found her other playground. Gently at first, he applied a little pressure nuzzling on the outside but then pushed, pressing a little harder, sinking into the centre, slipping through and inside her bottom. She enjoyed and welcomed the pressure of him there as she continued to raise and drop her body down onto him harder and faster each time. She was so tight around his finger but he managed to push it fully inside her and held it there as he could feel his penis stroking against it from inside.

Leaning back, she was reaching her ultimate sensation, climaxing, gushing her creamy, sticky love juice all over his penis as he continued. Now, as she had exhausted herself, he took control. As she came, he could feel her clenching tighter, constricting around him and he began to move his finger in and out of her bottom to intensify her climax and made her come again and again, longer and harder than she'd ever come before. He did this in time with the motion of her sitting herself on and off of his penis as she pulsated onto him, consuming him, becoming even more tight. Tighter, and climaxing like never before, made it harder for him to penetrate her and he too was struggling to control the compression. It was his turn now, coming to his own crescendo, spilling himself into her. Both pulsated out of control, eventually slowing to a steady rock and finally a halt.

She could feel his finger exiting her bottom and stroke her cheek as a way of saying thank you silently while she sat there for a moment, satisfied, able to feel the whole of his penis still erect but slightly relaxing inside of her. He held her waist and kissed her cleavage before she stood up from his lap.

After adjusting and straightening themselves, they left the room through the security door to rejoin the club where they continued to dance close to each other into the morning. He assisted her to walk the short journey home in daylight, linking his arm to steady her after dancing in her heels all night. They exchanged numbers and concluded the attraction was mutual and discussed casually, without conviction, the desire for an encore and would be in touch to arrange a rendezvous sooner rather than later, when it was convenient. They parted with a lingering soft kiss at her door and before long it was all a distant memory as she woke three hours later and prepared for work.

She was slow and lethargic to wake and slept through the alarm, so consequently would now be late. She fumbled and hurriedly tied her hair up in a bun, grabbed a coffee in a beaker, yanked open the door and, now in her Converses, sure-footed her way down the stairs and walked to the office. She skipped up the steps and entered the code to open the door. Walking into the building, she cheerfully greeted everyone with a smile and a "good morning" as she reached and sat down on her swivel chair, swung round and hauled herself into her desk where a pile of paperwork was waiting for her.

Setting her coffee down, she heard the boss shout out her name from behind the glass-panelled door. Looking round, she could see her beckoning her from behind her oversized boardroom table, sitting in her oversized chair in her air-conditioned office.

Oh dear, she thought, *what could I have possibly done to upset her now. I've only just walked through the door*. She pushed herself away from her desk, walked into the boss's office and stood there in front of her like a naughty schoolgirl with her hands behind her back and head facing the floor, waiting for the wrath. The boss looked first at her monitor, then at her with a disapproving, scowling face, then back to her monitor before she swivelled it round for her to take a look, take a *good look* at it for herself. It was the CCTV footage from the storeroom of the club last night, showing every graphic push, shove, thrust and pull from both of them with their erotic and what she thought private, performance.

Once she had witnessed what was on the screen, she gasped in horror. At first she felt embarrassed but then burst out with rapturous laughter, then nervous giggles before confessing,

'Oh, yeah, sorry, Mum, that's a guy I met downstairs last night. His name's Harrison and he's in the Royal Engineers, back from camp for the weekend. I've invited him for dinner this Sunday if that's OK?' She announced before she turned and started to walk out of the office, leaving the door open.

'Is that it?' Mum questioned in shock, shouting after her. 'Anastasia, the last thing I need to see is your ass on my CCTV footage from last night! If it happens again, I *will* be telling your father!' Mum paused and looked back at the monitor and sighed before shouted after her, 'Does he have any allergies?'

10

Detention

She stood nonchalant and unenthusiastic, with her arms crossed, holding a cup of coffee in one hand with a shoulder propped up against the edge of the wooden sash window, utterly bored on a cold, uneventful November afternoon. She observed but didn't perceive or take too much notice of the rain that was lashing down outside. It forcefully hit and chased its way down the small square single-glazed windowpanes, forming small droplets off each one before jumping off the window sill and dive-bombing into the muddy puddles that collected on the ground.

She quietly starred out, straight ahead at first, across to the far side of the playing fields in the distance, then glanced over and examined the flower and herb beds that sat underneath her classroom window. She scanned and inspected them, in search of something she wasn't sure of. Not really relating to any of it, she was uninterested and uninspired with every aspect of the view. Her thoughts couldn't have been further away – far from standing in her classroom, babysitting teenage delinquents.

All the while, the warmth and closeness of her breath on the glass panels was warming and misting up the inside. It allowed her to escape briefly as it obscured and made the view of reality hazy and disappear just out of focus for a moment. The yearning to be somewhere totally different was becoming more meddlesome and interfering with how she had been prioritising her life.

Her secret solicitations went rampaging inside her head like a riot. The passion for lust poisoned her entire body as it surged and pulsed through her bloodstream. Desperately trapped and isolated, she had no one to confide in or share her feelings with. She was wasting her efforts and emotions on someone she was captivated and spellbound by, so close but so far away, who was just across the hallway. He sat in the staff room, joyfully chatting to every single other female member of staff, who were all unmistakably flirting with him and him reciprocating the attention, blissfully unaware, not knowing that she even existed.

She wished she had the confidence, composure and ability to build a professional relationship with him then that could potentially create an opening for her to build a personal relationship with him afterwards. But all the while she stayed away, far away, far too shy to even attempt to approach him, scared of rejection, the notion she wasn't good enough. Why would he be the slightest bit interested in her? She flicked through all her thoughts of all the crazy fun they could have together, if she could only build up the courage to pursue him. She could feel the pounding of her heart erupting out of control while holding onto the tepid, untouched cup of coffee resting on her arm. Her tightly clenched fist held onto it as if her life depended on it.

She started to relax as she began to break out of her bubble of the daydream as she heard voices behind her once more coming from the staff room as it reached the end of tea break. She heard the laughing and chatting, incomprehensible white noise as they began to tip the remains of their coffee and tea in the sink, clanking and rattling the cups and mugs hurriedly into the dishwasher tray before herding out of the staff room, back to their classrooms for the last hour of torture before sending their student's home. She came to and placed her mug on the windowsill as the classroom once more filled with victims for her last lesson of the day; both her and they had no desire to be there either. Gathering her professional thoughts now, she began delivering the lesson.

Time passed sluggishly but then the buzzer pierced abruptly through the silence and, in the blink of an eye, crazed animals dressed in blue blazers spilled out of each classroom into the corridor. They scrambled and scattered, fleeing the school as if it had a disease they were unwilling to catch. Rolling like marbles out of the exits of the building, across the playground either on foot or by peddle power, they vanished through the gates, never to be seen again. Well, not until Monday morning.

It didn't take too long before the corridors fell silent once more and were returned to the teachers and staff as they were the only ones remaining after the flood of blue blazers were washed away. Her heels clip-clopped on each footstep loudly echoing on the polished wooden floor as she made her way down the vacant corridor to the resource cupboard, past *his* room. She glanced in as she walked by his window, slowing her pace deliberately so she could stare at him for just a little bit longer.

There he was, the finest specimen she had ever had the pleasure to be associated with.

Six-foot-four, tanned, tortoiseshell glasses, brown hair, naturally highlighted, flopping over to one side. He was an absolute tease without even knowing it. He was a natural, showing off his divine pert ass in those trousers as he bent over and, as he turned slightly, she just caught a glimpse of his front bulge. This was teamed with his tight-fitting shirt pulling over his biceps and chest gaping at the buttons slightly as he reached forward to the whiteboard, light pen in hand, recalibrating and organizing the schedule ready for Monday. She couldn't help but ogle him through the glass.

Her pace slackened gradually before she came to a complete stop right outside his classroom, staring directly at him through the glass panel. She was obsessed with him, it was almost as if she was stalking him, watching his every move, spying on him. He was a drug she got high on, needing a fix, infatuated by him. Now she was potentially steaming up another glass window but the difference, this time, was that she was very enthusiastic and exceptionally interested in the view on the other side of this glass panel.

Becoming flushed as the very thought of just talking to him, the sound of his voice, engaging in a conversation on a personal level, made her crazy with eagerness and made her burst with aspiration. It was undoubtedly the cause for her breathing to become like that of a racehorse galloping out of control, desperately trying to reach the finish line. She tried desperately to take control of her breathing and willed her legs to get walking again but, alas, she was unsuccessful and, oops, now it was too late. He turned his head and looked up to see who the slowing footsteps belonged to and she had been caught, staring straight at him. It was clearly inevitable she wasn't going to have to wait much longer to have that private conversation. He spotted her spying through the window, abandoning the whiteboard, with pen in hand, and swaggered towards her and was at the door turning the handle in a flash. He opened the door and just stood there like Adonis, one hand around the knob and the other resting on the frame as he greeted her with a smile. She definitely had no chance of escaping now, she was frozen, stuck to the spot, unable to move.

'Hello, Penny. How wonderful to see you. What can I do for you, do you need help with anything?' he asked politely in his delicate, friendly, endearing and gentlemanly voice.

She looked up at him, captivated by his creamy, tender tone and thought in her head, *OMG, Bradley, yes, yes you can bloody help me. I've got this relentless, unmerciful aching in my groin that I've had constantly for the last three months ever since you arrived and I believe that the only thing that could possibly and wholeheartedly satisfy it is the complete penetration of your huge cock deep inside of me. My fanny has been fluttering in waves, convulsing and gorging itself every time I encounter the smell of your aftershave, the sound of your voice. Even knowing you will be in work has put me into a state of uncontrollable emotions and multiple orgasms. Bend me over the filling cabinet in your stock cupboard at the back of the class and shag me from behind, you bastard...*

But, in reality, as her shy, nervous, delicate, unintrusive self, responded with, 'Hmm, well, ah... Hmm. Yes, silly of me, really...' she announced nervously as she tried to think of an excuse for why she would be gawking at him through his closed door. 'I've, ah, misplaced my, my charger for my whiteboard pen and wondered... do you had a spare I could borrow?' she asked awkwardly, lying through her teeth, trying to sound convincing. She could feel the fire flushing and engulfing her face and moving down her body as he looked at her tenderly.

He let go of the doorframe and began to walk back into his room, encouraging her to follow. 'Yes, of course, come, come in and I'll have a look for you, I'm sure I have a collection of them in my stock cupboard.'

He turned and casually swaggered back across the classroom, adjusting and tucking in a few untidy chairs as he went, to the back of the room after detouring and safely placing his own pen on his desk. Penny followed apprehensively, showing a shy and weary exterior but, raging deep beneath, she was engulfed with coarse and turbulent thoughts of uncultured and savage intentions.

They walked into the darkened stock cupboard. The celling lights were turned off as they never worked properly, only flickered when they were turned on, so he'd bought a spotlight lamp from home. Just a makeshift light which was perched at the far end of the cupboard on the middle shelf. The light enhanced and highlighted his silhouette and totally eclipsed her from sight. Shadowing her completely, it cast the shape of his body on the bare wall behind her. She couldn't see and was unaware he had already turned round to face her. She continued forward and walked straight into him. He took her hand, pulled it closer towards his toned abs, twisting her palm upwards and placed the charger securely in her hand and closed it.

Still holding her hand firmly, he looked mercifully and longingly at her, politely but seductively, and announced, 'But that's not what you really want... is it, Penny?' Holding her hand against his stomach, he hung there waiting respectfully for her response or a reaction, an answer to his forward question.

Penny looked up at him, startled, in utter shock and disbelief at what he had just done and said to her. *Did he really say that out loud? If he did it's out in the universe now, no going back.* Being in the cupboard, she didn't have to worry about her face flushing from embarrassment or the awkwardness of what other colleagues may think or say. The horse had started the race again. *What does he mean? OMG, has he secretly had feelings for me all this time but hid them behind a mask?* He obviously had a more convincing poker face than her. She tried to compose herself while the shortness of breath made her slightly giddy and lightheaded with exhilaration. The pulling flutters had multiplied into a frenzy of activity. Hysterical madness now ran through her veins with receipt of the evidence that he too may be interested in her. She blinked nervously, momentarily looking away, anywhere away from looking at him and committing to any intimate interaction. She had waited for him to notice her for so long. She looked down at the floor with a faint thought of embarrassment after what she had dreamed of doing to him up until now. She looked back up and replied calmly but slightly anxious of what the next step might be. 'No... no, it isn't.' Returning her glance to the ground and closing her eyes, she was ashamed of her honesty, laying it bare for him to ridicule... Maybe he meant did she want staples or Sellotape, A4 paper for the photocopier... *OMG!* Now she was scared of his response.

After loosening his grip and removing the charger from her hand and placing it back on the shelf, he guided her empty upturned hand round his side, turning it towards him and planting it firmly onto his butt cheek. Placing his other hand firmly round her waist, he sharply tugged her closer allowing their bodies to fully touch each other. She was taken by surprise and averted her eyes back to his.

The refined, delicate, respectful and polite Bradley melted away revealing a turbulent, uncultured, violent beast from within as he guided his hand from around her waist, down to her bottom before clawing it forcefully and thrusting it into his groin. He pushed up against her rubbing himself onto her as he bent down and gave her neck open-mouthed kisses, one after another, becoming more frantic with each kiss. The casket he had been secretly holding tightly locked was now open and he boiled over with uncontrollable lust. She was in shock; she had never seen this side of him before. Feverish with the need of urgency in case he had made a terrible mistake or was just joking with her, she immediately brought her other hand up to embrace the side of his face as she hurriedly elevated herself further up onto her tiptoes to reach his mouth. She ceased them and collided frantically, snaring his tongue in her mouth, tousling harshly.

He leant her against the shelving and dragged up one of her legs to the side of him as she mirrored her other leg, wrapping them around him the best she could as she pulled up her skirt so as not to rip any seams. He cradled and held her there as he spun her round, placing her down on to the top of a chest of drawers firmly. Fumbling up inside her skirt for her knickers, he grabbed both sides and dragged them down her thighs, loosening his grip momentarily as they snagged at her bent knees. After repositioning his hands once more, he tore them down past her ankles, finally discarding and throwing them to one side where gravity let them become free and fall to the floor. She wrenched up his shirt aggressively, liberating it from his tightly belted trousers as he tussled and fumbled with his belt and fly. She groped at his chest, searching and finding his nipples she had admired from afar. They made her erupt with desire while they hid beneath his cotton rich white shirts every single weekday since he started working there. She continued to play and teased them erotically underneath his shirt, making them as erect as his cock.

Free of his trousers, he pulled her in sharply. She could feel him on her bare skin, soft, smooth and hard, ready for play. With his hands on her bottom, it only took one more abrupt shove in his direction and he was in her. No hesitation, no foreplay, just an arrow embedding itself straight into the target, right to the top, bullseye. Hard and strong, the whole of him brashly inside her as fast and hard as he could muster, over and over again.

Her breath was taken as their groins clashed and jolted back and forth with furry against each other, desperately holding on, wanting the pleasure to last. Biting at his neck, she clutched at his arms as they clenched with strength, shoving and hauling her back and forth, on and off of him. She lent herself back so he could witness himself travelling deep inside as she swallowed him and then revealing and drawing himself out of her. Positioning and adjusting herself so he could press further and harder up against her G-spot on every thrust.

She ensnared him with the grasp of her legs as she hitched and linked them around him, heaving him closer as he shoved. He lost control and erupted into her with a vocal outburst of desire, which she accepted fully and graciously. They both embraced the moment and held on to each other tightly but calmly after the violent storm, this time with more caring tendencies as their breathing eased. As the moment passed, they composed themselves and he relaxed and felt the intensity, heat and softness of her as he retracted from inside her one last time.

Content after reliving the pent-up lust for each other, they redressed, straightened and returned to normality as their heartrates lowered. Now fully clothed, Penny walked towards the light from outside of the open stockroom door. Bradley reached out grasped her hand and pulled her back to hold her close, tightly nuzzling his face into her neck, inhaling her sweet perfume. Before his declaration.

'Young lady, you have been a very naughty girl and I refuse to tolerate this behaviour,' he said with a smirk and enthusiastic tone. 'You have earnt yourself detention every day next week. Report to my stock cupboard where I will administer appropriate punishment,' he addressed her authoritatively as he stroked his hands up and down her back and cuddled her close.

She pulled away from him with a smile and then kissed him delicately, lingering, before she walked out of the cupboard with him following close behind. Returning to the front of the classroom, he retrieved his pen from his cluttered desk as she walked through the classroom door, gently closing it behind her, glancing back and smiling widely. He returned the compliment with an open-mouthed smile and an added wink before continuing with his paperwork, knowing next week at school would be so much more stimulating, enjoyable and electrifying than this last week.

Who would have thought... the feeling was mutual.

11

Last Dance

Serenading of entities close to the touch,
Holding him firm as the floor they would dust.

Strength of his arms that clasped her aloft safely,
Confided the trust to not drop her or break thee.

In circles they glide as if skating on ice,
Compatible their feelings would suffice and be nice.

Swirling about while holding her tight,
She knew too well, not to put up a fight.

As music played loud with notes they both trust,
Round they would spiral, unsure if it's just lust?

Pulling her close only to brush her away,
Changing and shifting his mind, as they continued
to play.

Crashing like cymbals with an abrupt halt,
The feelings she sensed just was not her fault.

The tug of love or the thrust of lust,
What should she do as she desired to trust?

Being played before she knew only too well,
Not to attach, ponder, expect, overthink or dwell.

Just think fast on your feet, for a possible solution,
To get what you require or wished for, a final
conclusion.

The platform of lust which might forever be
changing,
Her struggle to reach could be challenging or
blaming.

Control, power, supremacy, overwhelming desire,
The raging of heat from the burning deep inside
her.

The music notes stopped and she wanted to bolt,
But for love nor money she was entrapped like a
cult.

Up against his body, skin firm to the touch,
She refused to let go, hand stuck fast to his butt.

They stood there like statues her face to his face,
Engulfed by his warmth and strength of embrace.

They'd pirouetted and shared years of sweet history,
Why they didn't make it work was an absolute mystery.

Each heartbeat raced through the sweat and the cloth,
Holding him close not wanting to stop.

Embracing him tightly, too scared to let go,
Should she just tell him, would he want to know?

He looked at her adoringly, wanting to dance more,
But regretfully distracted when hearing the door.

She came down to earth and released her grasp,
As in walked his girlfriend, she knew t'was her last.

12

OMG, You!

Why the hell do shops shut! she fumed as she hurriedly stormed down the walkway of the shopping centre on a mission. She was racing to get to the department store before the shutters slowly fell, descending to the floor and barricading everything in and forbidding anyone else to enter until tomorrow. She couldn't let this happen, she needed to get in there today – tomorrow would be just too late.

It was her own stupid fault; she should have just bought the dress yesterday when she was there with Jane. Jane, bless her, she even held it up and waved it, right in front of her face, under her nose, shaking and showing it off mouthing, *This is the one, it looks lovely on you.* But, as usual, she was so distracted and absorbed with work, talking to a client on her phone the entire time they were out shopping. She just glazed over and dismissed it totally, along with all the other dresses, flapping it away with her free hand and screwing up her face in loathing, as she finalised the deal on the phone.

So, Jane returned it to the rail just as she had done with all the other dresses she had attempted to show her that afternoon. Its only now Stephanie wished she had been more attentive while she had Jane there helping her like she always did and left her phone in the car or even in her bag on silent. Any of the above would have worked.

The shopping trip was organised weeks ago purely because Stephanie was always the friend that was so busy and so difficult to tie down. It was exceptionally hard as she was always travelling with her work, but her friends knew this and were always juggling their plans around to accommodate her schedules of clients, meetings and work trips.

Luckily for Stephanie, she could always count on Jane – she was an absolute gem. She'd always been and always would be the sensible and most practical one of the outfit. Jane was like her personal assistant in times like these, she was already on the case and took it upon herself to arrange for the staff to put the dress to one side until the end of tomorrow, which was today. She just knew Stephanie wouldn't be able to make time to organise or hunt down another alternative dress anywhere else for the birthday party tomorrow. It was an important one, it was Hayley's 50th, and because of this, the celebrations were due to start earlier. They would be bigger and more extravagant than they usually were for the average birthdays.

Stephanie invariably left absolutely everything to the last minute, mainly due to her overpowering and overbearing career. She was always organising and arranging everything down to the fine details for everyone else so *their* plans, lives and schedules could run smoothly like finely tuned racing cars. However, this left her personal life in an unorganised shambles, playing second fiddle in many aspects of her life. Having to cancel at the last minute, or always being late, created more problems. She never did invest the time to track down or pursue a man, settle or slow down enough to have any children. This gave the tendency for people to assume she may have actually been gay and scared to come out, shagging the boss, hiring prostitutes, but she dismissed those notions on every occasion. She had an entourage of boyfriends, one-night stands, those who wanted more, some needy, others overbearing, wanting her to settle as a wifey.

They all came but went when she unsympathetically or controllingly hung them up behind the door to concentrate on putting her career first.

All her friends adored and loved her dearly and were exceptionally happy for her and her amazing successful career and the ultimate perks. They got to join in the excursions and weekends away to lavish hotels in exotic countries, having fun, leaving their drab and repetitive lives behind them for a moment to have unadulterated fun. It was undeniable that some were a little envious as she still had her dynamite figure which she worked on vigorously at the gym. But she really didn't have much more than that; no husband, no children, only a lonely goldfish which swam around alone in its bowl in her apartment, waiting for her to feed it flacks and change its water once a week.

She relentlessly ran on that treadmill in the gym and at work, hungry for promotion and recognition, the need to be noticed by co-workers and work colleagues. She revelled in the attention and praise she received for meeting her deadlines, getting the results her boss craved. She accomplished all her targets and made the company look inviting and very appealing to prospective clients but, in the meantime, she sacrificed and neglected her personal life because of focussing solely on her achievements.

Most of her friendships unravelled and eventually slipped away from her in the process of her climbing and elevating up that ladder. However, a few remained loyal and durable enough to hang around to support her emotionally when she did find time in her busy schedule to socialise and have some fun. These were her true friends who she knew she could rely on, and they understood her impeccably.

So, holding three boutique bags with string handles threaded through her arm, while juggling a phone to her ear and her other hand carrying a large coffee, she galloped, getting ever closer to the store to complete her mission to collect the dress. *Going over in her head hurriedly, it's going to close, am I going to make it?* The closer she got to the deadline, the more she convinced herself she needed to have that particular dress. *I really want that dress, I really need that dress for tomorrow, for tomorrow, oh damn it, I didn't get a card.*

Her quest wasn't made any easier as she had come straight from the office where she had been working late, another deadline that needed to be finalised.

She could only take little steps and trot from wearing her four-inch stilettos, teamed with her tightly fitted short skirt that tugged at her thighs just above her knee, restricting every step simultaneously. Blinkered and self-absorbed with her eyes on the prize, she was aware of people walking around her but oblivious to anything important happening. She was totally unaware as a man began to emerge almost in slow motion from a shop to her left and continued to walk straight out in front of her.

She didn't acknowledge him until it was too late to put her brakes on and collided full frontal into his toned, tightly muscled shoulder. She came to an abrupt halt after impaling and winding herself onto him, while letting out an astonished shriek of surprise. On her impact she inadvertently squeezed the paper cup and the poorly fitting plastic lid shot off the top allowing the coffee caramel to erupt like a mini volcano, spraying out its contents high into the air. Her phone was knocked free of her hand and span in circles as it skated across the polished floor, eventually coming to a stop 20 feet in front of her.

What goes up must come down, as the saying goes, as did the coffee. Raining down, splattering all over them both, they stood there together in utter shock. It blotted and seeped into wherever it landed. His crisp white shirt soon was awash with poorly shaped coffee-coloured polka dots, and droplets fell down the side of his face. Her cerise chiffon blouse was ruined, as was her skirt. Like statues they just stood there looking at the mess created by their collision, waited for the shower to finish before slowly looking at each other, stunned. They made eye contact, still in shock, looking at each other in disbelief, searching for the right words to use for an appropriate answer to the question they were both thinking. An apology maybe. Who was to blame for the collision?

She was not happy at all and scowled up at him ready to give him a piece of her mind, to lecture him on his incompetence, negligence and disregard for not looking where he was going. She took a deep breath and opened her mouth, ready to start, but stopped dead in her tracks. Her face softened as her eyes opened with shock and surprise as she began to recognise the familiar face standing there in front of her, covered from head to toe in her coffee.

She hadn't seen him since... since she finished with him when they were 17. Stunned but bemused as the same time, they both just stared straight at each other, into each other's eyes up close, captivated at first, slowly braking into a smile then nervous out-of-breath giggles and laughter as they realised who it was. Taken aback, she bent over and started to brush her skirt with her coffee-drenched hands, looking up occasionally but mainly averting her eyes to the ground, wishing it would open up and swallow her whole so she could escape from him once more. She really didn't want to be there in the company of him again.

Looking back up at him momentarily and hearing him erupt with laughter nervously, also in shock, she recalled in a flash, remembering how much enjoyment they had encountered when they were together as teenagers. While the coffee trickled down his now slightly weathered but still dreamy face that she used to hold and call her own, she thought instantly that she never did want to call it off but she had to accept the reality of a strict upbringing and had no choice but to conform to the rules and regulations of family and the obligation to carve out a career.

The memories unnerved and hit her like an unforgiving wave crashing into her just as abruptly as they had just collided. Taking her breath away she struggled to compose herself, breathing heavily and fast through the shock and delight of seeing him after being separated for what seemed a lifetime. It disturbed all these emotions that had been sleeping, lying dormant inside her for so long. Now she was feeling fuzzy and fluttery, warm and joyful, in seeing him after all this time.

She was initially shocked but then her mind was flooded with loving thoughts of him. It all immediately consumed her, taking her back to when they were young, tugged at all of her emotions and memories with no sign of stabilising or easing. Maybe it was a cruel trick or just fate. As if by magic, someone had scooped him up, fast forwarded time and dropped him back down so he appeared in front of her 33 years later.

Whatever it was, she was somehow grateful, feeling thankful and glad of it.

'Hello, Tea.' He spoke softly and calmly once he had stopped laughing but still looked a little shocked. He was attempting to comprehend that his first love was standing there, larger than life, right in front of him, who he hadn't seen since the late '80s. He instantly remembered her pet name.

'Good evening, Choc,' she replied after a deep breath, with a smile and a hint of sarcasm and confidence. There was no question as to who dumped who but now seeing, him after all this time, she was intrigued by how handsome he still was and began to feel a little bit regretful. Why, why did she let him go? Oh, those pet names were cringe now but they stuck.

'I am sooooo sorry,' he apologised as he ran, retrieved and delivered the phone back into her empty upturned hand tenderly.

'No, no, not at all, it was totally my fault. I'm so sorry, I should have been looking where I was going. Are you all right, you're not burnt anywhere, are you?'

As she apologised, she automatically touched his chest, gently and softly stroking him to try to ridiculously brush the blotted coffee marks off his shirt, which had obviously completely absorbed into the fabric. Being totally unsuccessful, she slowed her stroke and retracted her hand away awkwardly as she comprehended she had been stroking his chest, enjoying it just as much as the shirt over it. The coffee had stained fast in elongated oval patches, now looking more like pebbles and were destined never to be separated, a permanent feature. She went back and began, this time, brushing over his stomach.

He observed her hand rubbing back and forth for a moment before he reached out and caught hold of it as it skated and padded over his stomach frantically trying but failing miserably to erase the now soaked in coffee. She surrendered and stopped when she became ensnared in his monster-size hand that engulfed her tiny fragile fingers. He would have quite easily snapped them off if he wanted to hurt her or had applied any pressure to his grasp. Not having felt his touch for such a long time she was taken aback by his tender, delicate and refined catch that secured her in front of him.

Without a word spoken from his mouth, his eyes screamed volumes to how much he had missed her and how overjoyed he was to have her standing in front of him once more, holding her hand, close to him, her touching him after being absent from his world for what seemed like an eternity. He had missed her terribly and thought about her endlessly over the years. So much regret and so many questions to ask her.

The dormant embers that laid inside her that she had carried since they were together had reignited abruptly. Little sparks and electric shocks of delight erupted and raced like space dust, tingling all over her body uncontrollably. She had totally forgotten what it felt like to be so up close and personal to him. So close she could smell his aroma disguised faintly by the stains of coffee. She realised how good he smelt, recognising it was the aftershave she had introduced him to all those years ago. He was still wearing it after all these years.

They were entrapped, entranced by each other, locked in their individual thoughts that swirled in their minds separately. But they knew what the other was thinking as if they were both telepathic. His adrenaline pumped through his veins and with her hand held close to his body, she could feel his heartbeat wildly out of control. She reminisced in that moment what they were and what they had so long ago, had never been replicated since, it was unique. Everybody could see it and spoke about it, but they maybe took advantage of it and abused its fragile balance, unaware of what they actually had until it had gone.

Then, suddenly, he retracted away from her and released her hand. It fell helplessly down, lifeless with no resistance to gravity and hung there by her side. She was devastated and confused that he had let her go. Bewildered, she searched with scared eyes, frustrated as to why he had let go so hurriedly She didn't understand. Forbidden to continue or unable to sustain her gaze any longer, she felt savagely torn away.

It all became clear, this time by the disturbance of a nagging, screeching voice coming from a short scruffily dressed woman walking towards them out of the same shop he came out of moments earlier, dragging two unruly small children with her, one in each hand, desperately attempting to control them. It was his wife, hurling insults, spitefully and relentlessly, shouting directly in his face. Like bullets, the abuse flew out of her mouth pointed unswervingly at him, hitting him at point-blank range. She pummelled and buried him into the ground with venomous words, with no mercy or break to draw breath. The reason for her anger seemed to be because he left her to supervise the children so he could look at something he wanted to see.

She was utterly surprised and astonished by this woman's animosity, aggression and disrespectfulness towards him. She seemed to be oblivious that he was covered from head to toe in coffee and that he was talking to someone as she commanded him to hurry up. They both watched as she turned and began to walk away from them and headed out of the shopping centre into the car park, dragging the children behind her.

No that can't be... can it? That's not... Caroline? She used to be the most happy-go-lucky, thin, attractive, petit and toned person when she knew her, destined to be a highflyer and very successful lawyer. Thankfully their paths never crossed much so she probably wouldn't have recognised Stephanie from Adam, thank God.

Everyone wanted to date Caroline when they were younger but now, wow, she has blossomed into a vulgar coarse hag with a violent temper, with no regard for Paul. Whereas he had become a downtrodden, under-the-thumb shadow of the man he used to be. He endured the torture until she felt the need to take a breath or stamped her feet to get her own way, it seemed.

They both watched as she walked away into the distance until it became silent and peaceful once more. In shock, and he being humiliated by his wife yet again, they both turned back to one another. Embarrassed, he shrugged his shoulders, raising his eyebrows and looked down at the floor, before he turned away and followed his wife, returning to his miserable existence. And just like that he left, swiftly chasing after his wife to catch up with her, no doubt to be subjected to more verbal abuse. Astonished by the whole experience, astounded at what he had become, she too began to turn away from him, only glancing back once. Then she continued on her original quest, walking in her original direction this time less rushed, slowly and still slightly stunned by the whole scenario.

The only thing racing and galloping now were the thoughts in her head about Paul and how he had changed so much. Inspecting her phone, she thumbed through the contacts, searching with no luck, wishing she had kept his number logged.

She approached the store that held her dress and thought was that it, that was all they were going to have, after being apart for so long. Her thoughts were rudely interrupted as she felt someone grasping her from behind, holding onto her arm frantically, tugging her backwards. Startled by the force, she turned back quickly to investigate who it was. Was she being robbed? To her surprise, it was Paul, slightly out of breath as he had run back to her after excusing himself from his wife with the thought he may have lost his wallet when bumping into her. Her heart quickly skipped a beat and filled with joy once more, exhilarated with the relief that he came back. But why?

Holding her arm in one hand, he urgently grabbed her other shoulder, drew her forward and coarsely kissed her on her lips, not even giving her a chance to accept it graciously, close her eyes, pucker up or receive it in any other way than hastily and unrefined. Letting her go, he held out his business card and thrust it swiftly into her hand with the hope she would take it. Turbulently, with a sense of urgency in his voice he requested, 'Call me, please, please, call me tomorrow.' Then he turned and ran away, back to his wife, without looking back to acknowledge her. Once again, he was gone, and she was alone.

Now as she was abandoned, left on her own, she looked down at the business card he frantically placed in her hand and read it in her mind before announcing joyfully out loud with a contented smile, 'OMG, he always wanted to be an architect. He made it.'

Oh boy, what to do next. He had just come out of nowhere and now the feelings she had buried long ago were bubbling up to the surface erupting and spilling over uncontrollably. Long-lost memories returned, catapulted to the front of her mind, demanding immediate attention. *Is this a Pandora's box full of unfinished business, longing to be opened?* Should she address it or drop the card there and then, walk away very quickly, not looking back, just as he did. She looked down longingly at it, undecided and in a quandary, holding it in one hand, chasing her fingers delicately over the raised lettering of his name, around the edge, before holding and tapping it repetitively on her fingernails. She stared at the front and then flipped it over to view the back, almost as if she was looking for a solution, a response to her query. *What should I do?*

Looking back far into the distance where he had disappeared, she gently lowered the card respectfully into the sides of one of the bags she had hooked back on to her arm. Still unsure of what to do, she turned and continued to walk towards the store, then tuned one last time, desperate to see if he would appear again before she reached the entrance of the store and stepped inside. Just in time, the security guard was poised with his key in the shutters, getting ready for the ten-minute warning announcement of closure to the customers.

The wings of her butterflies were fluttering around crazily, wanting to escape from inside her, to be free and scream out to the world how she felt about him. Obviously, there was definitely something still there. The fire had been started, with no warning of its intensity, and was being stoked by the wonderful memories flooding back of their intimacy only they knew. Her breathing became brisk as her chest strained to contain her anticipation and excitement, her heartbeat increasing. She struggled to respectfully compose herself while trying to concentrate on collecting the dress for the party. All the time her mind was rebuilding the turbulent and uncultured building blocks of all the fun they had shared, along with the reckless passion and delight they gave each other for many years. This dilemma would have never had returned if he hadn't have walked out of the shop and cracked the surface of her streamlined existence. And, also, if she had paid attention to Jane yesterday and just bought the dress.

Young, energetic, more stamina than a prize stallion, and hung like one too. She began to blush as a smirk ran across her face, her eyes widened and sparkled with pure delight after reminiscing in her dirty little mind about all the landmarks they achieved together. She was regretful, utterly disgusted and disappointment with herself, for disregarding him and dismissing all those wonderfully naughty facts, totally erasing all of them from her hard drive.

Sailing round the department store on a high, she gazed at all the clothes that hung beautifully on the rails, touching and brushing her outstretched fingertips past the soft fabrics, as she made her way leisurely to the counter to collect her dress. She thought of his body and how she would touch and be touched by him, be close to him, if she had the chance, how she used to caress him softly in public, but in private they both totally changed into wild obsessive predators. Passionate, vigorous, harsh, savage loving.

She had put him on that pedestal, raising him up high, so high that he became a trophy, an Adonis, only being bought down on special occasions when needed, and to be polished, before placing him back up on the shelf for safe keeping. She had forgotten the pleasure, they gave each other as she steadily fell into the entrapment of work and business meetings, deadlines, impossible statistics for profits. Becoming greedy and hungrily pursuing the next promotion, unbeknown to her, the firm entrapped her. They added more shackles, claiming her as their slave. She worked all hours, running on that relentless wheel rather than spending precious time with him, robbing her of building their own portfolio called life. Suffocating her, as she became addicted to the buzz, making it impossible for her to kick the habit or escape from their hold.

She collected her dress and thanked the tiny, hunched lady behind the counter who recognised her from the visit yesterday. The lady smiled sweetly up at her and wished her a wonderful time at the party tomorrow.

Oh dear, the party. She walked around searching for the signs to show her where the greeting card section in the store was located. She hunted through and found an appropriate card, bought it and returned home where there was a rather large bottle of wine waiting for her to crack open in the fridge. She plucked the business card out of the bag and put it on the coffee table then laboured on how to possibly invite Paul to the party tomorrow without him knowing or cottoning on to the fact that she was so, so desperate, hungry to see him, to be touched by and be in his company once more.

She poured a large glass of wine and slumped down on the sofa, raised and poised the rim of the glass at her lips, looking at the phone in her other hand and the business card on the low coffee table in front of her. She pondered what to do, and how to invite him. What should she say?

'Why, why did he kiss me? How am I going to complete this challenge, what am I going to do?' she asked as she looked out into the empty quiet room with only an audience of one, her goldfish, Bubbles, pouting in her bowl at the side of the sofa. She imagined her friends on the other end of the sofa, listening to and coaching her on how to resolve this dilemma. But, as usual, the reality was she had to sort this one out herself, alone. No one must know just yet of her encounter. Should she call him, should she ignore him, oh what to do. *Oh, I don't know, what about his wife?* Did she really care about her... no, not really, well, it didn't look like it.

After a while, mesmerised by Bubbles and a few sips of wine, she made up her mind and started to tap frantically on her phone, writing a text, short and brief, straight to the point, no beating around the bush. He would either respond to it or not.

As least this way she would know which direction she was heading in or whether it was a knee-jerk reaction from him. She paused for a while, thinking of all her conquests, before she pressed the send arrow, anxiously watching it disappear into cyber space from the writing box and up into the screen of her phone to be logged in his inbox. She watched as the one tick turned to two ticks. Delivered. Nervously waiting, she watched the ticks turn blue; he had opened it immediately. With a sharp intake of breath, now all she could do was watch and wait for him to take the next step. Her hand started to shack with exhilaration as she witnessed the message "typing" appear in the top bar.

OMG. He's replied and sent a message back straight away.

She opened it, bursting with delight. A full open smile of intrigue and blissful cheerfulness overwhelmed her as she read it.

Next book is titled

OMG.

Author's Note

Life experiences mould you into who you are, be them nasty or nice, and the road you travel has its unexpected dramas, twists and turns, and can be utterly exhausting at times. I can't change the opportunities missed or lost through insufficient backing or lack of encouragement, but am grateful I never gave up on me.

I have been subjected to bullying throughout my entire life from a young age until present, deemed fat and sensitive, stupid and thick, with depression and anxiety that visited every so often.

As a child I sat at the back of the classroom, mainly being ignored by most if I wasn't being teased or laughed at by others. However, this is where I looked out of the window, being allowed to daydream, where I was left alone and felt my happiest and safest. I was always slow to grasp academia, struggled to keep up or stay focused and always missed play because I had to correct my spellings. It was in the '70s and there wasn't the extensive testing back then as there is today to find answers to questions asked.

But now I am an independent, strong woman who has overcome so many challenges and achieved so many things I thought I would never have the courage to even start, which has made me scared of nothing and openminded to embrace everything that has been thrown at me.

Writing is my escapism and I've never published a book until now.

I'm surrounded by precious people who love me and want the best for me, I wouldn't change any of it for the world.

Never give up hope and never give up on yourself.

In aid of Ovacome, the UK's
ovarian cancer support charity.

charity number 1159682
ovacome.org.uk

Love **passion** *adoration* LUST *purpose*

exploring gentle Caresse **caring** *flirty*

LOVINGLY *passionately* Stroke

feel adore COMFORT *thrust* Pleasure

explore adventure worthy **nipples**

manhood *fiery* possessive playful

tease *lustful* laughter enchanting

captivating *enhance* EROTICALLY **Love**

erotic *flirty* laughter chattering

POWERFUL **comfortable** lust *cares*

occasion ADVANTAGE **excitement**